The Billionaire's Baby

Axel and Chastity book 3

Lexie Miers

Chapter 1

Chastity

TWO WEEKS HAD PASSED SINCE I'D SPOKEN TO MY MOM, AND I WAS dying to tell her our good news. My baby was healthy, and my mom was going to have a granddaughter. I hoped she'd be happy for me. But I didn't want to just call up and blurt it out. Not like the initial announcement.

I wanted to do it right this time and tell her face to face.

This called for some planning. I called my dad and coordinated with him to organize a dinner for all four of us. Axel and I would meet him and Mom at a restaurant in the city.

When that Saturday arrived, Axel sent a car to get me and I met him at his apartment so I could shower, wash my hair and change into an outfit more suitable for a nice dinner.

"I can't believe how nervous I am," I told him while I was applying my lip gloss in the bathroom, my stomach aflutter with butterflies.

I'd bought a new simple black dress that was flowy around the boobs and waist. My tummy was starting to pop, and I was almost fifteen weeks now. Nothing fit me right, especially around the waist, so new clothes seemed like the best option.

"You look beautiful," Axel said from behind me, and I glanced up in the mirror to where his reflection was staring at me.

"And you're beyond handsome," I said, sighing at how amazing he looked in a simple pair of slacks and a shirt. Even without a tie or structured jacket, his shoulders were broad and gorgeous.

Axel flicked his wrist up and glanced at his watch. "We should go. You ready?"

"Yeah." I checked my reflection once more, then lifted my hand to stare down at my ring wrapped around the ring finger on my right hand. "I'm not sure I've ever really told you how much I love my ring. I wear it every day and I've never taken it off."

"Never?" he asked, coming forward to stand behind me.

I shook my head slowly, leaning into his warmth and staring at his face reflected in the mirror. "Never." Not even when I thought we would break up and I was so angry at him for missing the sonogram I could barely breathe.

He kissed my hair. "Let's go."

We went down to the garage in the elevator and got into his car.

"Still nervous?" he asked as I folded my hands together over my stomach.

"Absolutely."

"Why?" he asked. "Are you worried your mom will start another fight?"

"Oh, she definitely will," I told him with a grin. "That's just her way. With both you and Dad there tonight, I can only imagine what she's gonna say."

Her pregnancy hormones were most likely all over the place. Mine were still kicking my butt. The sickness had all but gone, but I was snappy, teary and horny. What a combination.

"Then if it's not that, what is it?" Axel asked as we drove out the garage door and towards the restaurant.

"It's just..." I sighed, trying to think about the right way to put it. "I think I just worry that she won't want to know about our baby. That she'll decide it's all too difficult and she doesn't want to be a grandma."

Hot tears filled my eyes and I waved at them while blinking rapidly. I was wearing more makeup than usual, and I didn't want it ruined and running down my face.

"I doubt that will be her response," Axel said. "But even if it is, I've heard things change once the baby arrives."

I glanced across the interior at him. "How do you know that?" I'd read the same thing, but how had he heard of it?

Axel shrugged as he pulled into a valet spot outside the restaurant and turned off the ignition. "I'm twenty years older than you, sweetheart. I've had friends have babies fifty times over. One of my best buddies had a baby before he finished high school, so I know a lot of stories and one of the main themes has always been that no matter how the parents react when they find out about the pregnancy, they're very different when they have a real baby to hold and love."

He reached across and picked up one of my hands, bringing my fingers to his lips to kiss. "So don't worry, things will work out, especially once they see our baby girl."

"You haven't told my father we're having a girl yet, have you?"

He shook his head. "No. I wasn't sure you wanted to share that with anyone."

The valet rushed over to the car, so we both got out.

Axel tossed the keys to the guy who looked about my age, and we headed into the restaurant.

"I thought we would tell them tonight," I said. "Since we know the results were pretty much one hundred percent accurate, why not?"

The IPSI test made me feel a lot better about thinking of our baby as a girl. We hadn't talked names or anything like that yet, but I was feeling more comfortable every day with the little being growing inside me.

I tucked my hand into the crook of Axel's elbow, and he glanced down at me. "Okay. Let's do it."

We walked into the restaurant, and I glanced around. It was spectacularly beautiful, with dimmed lighting, white tablecloths and classical music tinkling in the background.

"This place is lovely." I sighed.

"I thought it would be nice to go somewhere we could talk and hear each other," Axel said, and the maître'd took our name then escorted us over to a round table with four seats.

"Yes, it's definitely quiet," I all but whispered. There were only about ten tables in the whole place, and everyone was quietly sipping on their wine and eating their food. Slowly.

It was a little strange, and a stark comparison to the cafeteria I ate at every day, with conversation at a dull roar and clanking plates and silverware.

I was just about to ask Axel more about his new managerial team when my parents walked into the room.

I waved at them, and they smiled at me as they walked over. There was no running or hugging, or any of the elation I'd hoped for in my daydreams about this moment. But they'd come. That was the important thing.

"Hi, Mom. Hi, Dad."

They both smiled and sat, Mom next to me, my father next to Axel.

Axel stood up and shook my father's hand, but it was all a little stilted for me.

"Congratulations, Katherine," Axel said, looking at my mother. "How are you feeling?"

She brushed her hair back behind her ear and sighed. "Well, nervous. We have our twelve-week sonogram this week, and more blood tests."

"Why are you nervous, Mom?" I asked, then a horrible thought occurred to me.

What if something was wrong with their baby? How could we ever be happy if my mom lost hers? It would destroy my parents and us.

She cleared her throat. "You know. The doctors keep referring to my age like it's some sort of disease, and I'll feel a lot better once the amniocentesis is done. Did you have to have one of those?"

She looked straight at me, and I faltered.

"Oh, ah…"

"No, I don't think you did," Axel said. "You just had the blood test, right?"

I nodded. "Yes, we got the IPSI done."

"Oh?" Mom asked, her tone dead serious and nowhere near sounding like my mother. "How did it go?"

I grinned at her and glanced over at Axel, who nodded at me.

"It went really well. The baby's healthy, no anomalies to speak of, and we found out the sex."

"Oh, we don't want to know. Please don't tell us," she said, shaking her head and grabbing my dad's hand above the table.

"Um, okay," I said, feeling my heart fall sickeningly low inside my chest.

I glanced over at Axel, at a total loss now. Why wouldn't they want to know?

Axel turned back to my parents. "Are you two finding out what you're having? Or would you rather not?"

"Oh, we'll find out," Mom said. "But we won't tell anyone. I think that should be kept private, until the day the baby arrives, and then you can announce it."

I was flabbergasted. What a ridiculous thing to say to us.

I glanced over at my father, who was looking apologetic and worried. Then he turned to Axel. "Shall we order some wine?"

"Definitely."

Axel lifted his hand and a waiter hurried over and took their order. Mom and I ordered sparkling water.

To distract myself from the crippling disappointment within my heart, I picked up the menu, looking for the prices.

There were none.

"Axel..."

"Just order anything you'd like."

"But..." I hated not knowing how much anything cost.

He reached for my hand and did his hand kissing trick.

I slowly relaxed and returned to looking at the menu. I was starving, and low in iron. I didn't really feel like red meat, but I needed it.

"I think I'll go with the steak. Can you recommend which one would be the best?"

"Absolutely."

Suddenly my mom piped up, obviously seeing my issue with the menu. "How are we supposed to know what this is going to cost if there are no prices?"

I sighed and glanced at Dad. This was fun.

"Dinner's on me," Axel said smoothly. "I owed Pat dinner from his fortieth, and I thought we could double up with the joint celebration of our babies."

My mother's aggravated frown said it all, but at least she kept whatever was whirling inside her head to herself.

The waiter came by, and we managed to order even though she asked twenty questions and ended up requesting a meal that wasn't really on the menu anyway.

When that was finally done, I really felt like a drink but that wasn't going to happen. Not for a while yet.

I decided to steer the conversation into hopefully safer waters. "Axel, how's the new management team going? I didn't get to ask you before we came in."

"Management team?" my dad repeated.

Axel shifted on his chair, seemingly uncomfortable. Hadn't he told my father about this team yet?

"Well, I was going to ask you about it, actually Pat. On our run tomorrow."

"Ask what?"

"Well," Axel began, and glanced over to me. I wasn't sure what he was about to say because he hadn't told me anything yet.

"Well, it was pointed out to me by a few people who shall remain nameless, that I'm a bit of a workaholic."

Patrick chuckled and picked up his glass of red wine. "Can't argue that."

"So, Cheryl at my office has been working on hiring me a group of managers to take over some of my work, which will leave free me to pursue new accounts and perform the executive tasks that I prefer."

I watched my father's face as Axel spoke, and his surprise was obvious.

"Seriously?" Dad asked. "You're hiring managers to take some of your responsibilities?"

"He's delegating," I said with a grin.

My dad's eyebrows dropped. "I know that, I'm just surprised."

Axel reached over and grabbed my hand, threading our fingers and holding my hand where everyone could see. "I want to slow down for Chastity and the baby. I want to be able to be there for her when she needs me."

"How many managers are we talking about?" my father asked, his tone very business-like considering Axel had just said the most amazing thing about his dedication to me and our baby.

"I've hired three so far. All graduates from the same year."

"Oh, that's right," I said, joining in the conversation. "You mentioned Taylor wanted you to interview some of her classmates."

"Yes," Axel said, grinning at me. "And it's working out fantastically. They're all specialized and work really well together."

"So, what did you want to talk to me about?" Dad asked.

Axel squeezed my hand. "I haven't actually mentioned it to anyone yet, but would you consider coming to work with me?"

I glanced over at my mom, whose eyebrows had narrowed.

"In what capacity?" my father asked. "Because we always said we wouldn't work together."

I squeezed Axel's hand. "You and Dad have wanted to work together before?"

He nodded. "Yeah, we always said it wouldn't work. But since we're sort of family now, I thought I'd ask."

I gaped at him. Oh, God, Mom was gonna have a fit over this.

Chapter 2

Axel

THE TENSION AROUND ME WAS WORSE THAN THE MOST HOSTILE takeover meeting. What had I said that was so wrong that everyone at the table was looking at me like I was insane?

"What's wrong?" I asked.

Patrick shook himself as thought getting rid of bad thoughts. "In what capacity?"

"As my second in command," I said.

I'd been thinking about it a lot, and it didn't make sense why Pat couldn't work for me. He was terrific at what he did. "You'd oversee all the new managers I've hired. They're mid-twenties and could use your experience to coach them and keep them from doing anything stupid."

"Tell me about them," Pat requested.

I gave him a quick rundown of the three new hires. Two women and a guy. Between them, they spoke a half dozen languages and specialized in business, finance and economics.

"I'll come by tomorrow and meet them, if that works for you." Patrick's face was thoughtful, his eyebrows drawn together.

"There's no pressure. You don't have to say yes," I told him. "But I need more managers, and you'd be a perfect fit. But if you don't think you can work with me—"

"You mean *for* you, right?" Katherine interrupted, correcting me.

I slid my gaze over to the woman who'd twice managed to get accidentally pregnant by my best friend, twenty years apart. "Sorry?"

"You keep saying you want Patrick to work with you, but you mean you want him to work under you."

I frowned at Pat's partner and Chastity's mom. What was wrong with her? "I'm offering my best friend a job that he would be brilliant at and pays twice as well as his current position."

I was rounding down, actually. My new managers made more than Pat, and I'd pay twice their salary for an executive manager of his skill and work ethic. I'd never offered before because we'd made an agreement not to mix our friendship with business. But it didn't make sense anymore. Not with our current familial connections.

Chastity squeezed my hand. "That's so thoughtful of you, Axel. Thank you."

I could see she was grateful, and I wasn't going to say it out loud now, not with Katherine out for blood, but it had been Chastity's recommendation that I look at her father for a manger that had me thinking about it again.

"I should have done it years ago," I admitted, feeling a little embarrassed now. I probably should have offered him the job at a different time. When we were alone or over the phone, so he had time to think it over.

"Why didn't you?" Katherine shot out. "Or, maybe the question is, why are you offering now? For Chastity's benefit? Because it's not for ours."

"Kaiti..." Pat whispered at his partner, staring at her with a grimace rippling over his face.

Katherine just glared back at him.

I sat up straighter, regretting the offer completely now. "Look, I didn't mean to upset anyone. Maybe we can talk about this another time, Patrick?"

"Yeah. Good idea."

Chastity took her hand out of mine and reached for her soda. "What's your problem, Mom?"

Uh-oh. "Um, Chastity, maybe we should leave it."

"No. I want to know." Chastity stared at her mom. "Well?"

"Well, what?" Katherine barked back, her glare now trained on her daughter.

"What's your problem tonight? You know there's no paid maternity leave in America, right? So why wouldn't you encourage Dad to get a better job? A higher paying job?"

That was a good point, but I wasn't sure it was one Katherine was going to consider.

"You don't need to concern yourself with our finances, Chastity," Katherine snapped, sticking her nose in the air. "We're perfectly fine, thank you. A lot more comfortable than we were when we had you."

"Good," Chastity said. "Then you won't guilt this baby into thinking it's his or her fault you don't get to do anything."

Whoa. Okay. "Sweetheart…"

Luckily for me, since I had no idea what I was about to say next, two waiters turned up with our dinners, serving all four of us at once.

I stared down at my prawn risotto and picked up my fork. This was now awkward as hell.

"Enjoy your meals," the waiter said, and left.

Katherine's eyes were flaming with anger. "How dare you?" she hissed at Chastity.

Chastity's hand tightened into a fist on the table before she hissed back, "How dare I what?"

"How dare you think you can tell us what to do. You're the one who's repeating all the same mistakes we did, and you think you know better. Well, you don't. You barely know this man, and you're too young to have any baby, let alone his. There. I said it."

Katherine threw herself back in her chair and crossed her arms over her chest.

I stared at her with my mouth open.

Then I glanced across to where Chastity was beginning to boil with anger. Her face was flushing redder and redder.

I looked straight at Pat and wished I could whisper to him, *"What the fuck do we do?"*

But he was just staring at me with the same hopeless feeling I had pushing through my chest.

Did I intervene, or did I let this blow up the way it was meant to?

Maybe I could offer Chastity some support or help. "Sweetheart…"

Chastity pushed herself to her feet and glared down at her mother. "So, you think I'm too young to have this baby? Well, I'm older than you were with me! And in a thousand times better financial position, so you are wrong, Mom. Totally wrong."

"You should be going to chiropractic school, Chastity. Chasing your dream. Not letting one mistake ruin your future."

"Ah—" I started to interject, but Chastity exploded beside me.

"This isn't a mistake!" she practically screamed in the quiet restaurant. "You're the one making mistakes, getting pregnant at forty-three! But I at least supported you."

Katherine got to her feet too, not to be outdone by her daughter's theatrics. "This baby is our second chance. To be together, to be a real family."

I glanced across at Pat and saw the hurt in his face that I knew would be mirrored in Chastity's. She'd always felt like she was a burden to her parents, and now her mother was telling her that she was finally getting the baby she wanted.

I reached for Chastity's hand, but she shook me off.

"You and me, Mom—we're done. Enjoy your baby, because you're never going to get to see this one. She's just a mistake, anyway." Chastity cupped her belly, framing her swelling stomach with her hands. "Axel, let's go."

My stomach grumbled with hunger, but this place didn't do takeout meals. So, as Chastity grabbed all her stuff and twisted around to stomp towards the door, I followed her.

I made sure the maître'd knew the dinner was on me, instructing him to use my corporate account they had on file then followed Chastity outside, into the cool night air.

She was standing on the sidewalk breathing heavily, tears in her eyes.

"Are you okay?" I asked her, though it was obvious that she wasn't.

Chastity swiped at her eyes. "Did you hear what shhheee said?"

Her voice was wobbling as she spoke and it broke my heart to see her like that, but surely, she had to see what I saw. That her mother was just acting out irrationally. It didn't mean anything in the long run.

"Of course, I did, but she's just upset. And hormonal. I'm sure she's going to regret what she said to you, so please don't be angry. You can't take everything she says to heart." I glanced back into the restaurant and saw Pat walking out to us.

I leaned forward and pulled open the external door for him. He walked straight through and grabbed his daughter, pulling her into his arms. "I'm sorry, Chastity."

Chastity broke into sobs then and Patrick squeezed her tight.

I took a step back so I could look through the glass doors and see Katherine inside the restaurant. She was still sitting at her table, alone, mechanically chewing as though she were trying to enjoy her meal.

She probably is. The food here is delicious.

Pat pulled back, holding onto Chastity's upper arms. "I have to get back in there before she blows another valve. The doctor said her blood pressure's too high already and we have to keep her calm."

Chastity sobbed out a laugh. "Good luck with that."

Pat held out his hand to me. "I appreciate the job offer and I'll be over tomorrow, around one pm, if that's okay?"

I shook his hand and nodded. "I'll clear the schedule. Thank you."

My best friend nodded and went back into the restaurant.

I turned to Chastity. "Let's go and get something to eat, sweetheart. And you can tell me why you're so upset."

"Because," Chastity began, then stopped, swallowing awkwardly. "Because…"

She couldn't speak, so I gave the valet the card for our car and took her hand. "Where would you like to go for dinner? We can go anywhere you want."

She sniffed and wiped at her eyes, "Anywhere?"

"Anywhere." I may regret the offer later, but I could always order in something if I was still hungry.

My car pulled up in front of us and the driver got out and tossed me the keys. "Where to, beautiful?"

I opened her door and made sure she was buckled in before I rounded the hood. Once settled in my seat, I glanced over at my beautiful girl, who was red and smudged, and who I loved more than anything in the world.

"Home," she said.

"Uh, which home?" I asked, because that could mean her dorm, the apartment, my apartment or her mom's house.

Chastity laughed softly. "Can we go back to your apartment, order in some Thai food and eat in bed?"

There was a twinkle in her eye that I hadn't seen in months. "Of course. Let's go!"

"What do you want?" she asked, pulling out her phone and ordering via a phone app.

I mentioned a few appetizers and main dishes, then Chastity tapped it all in and sent the order off. "Great. Should be at our place in about half an hour."

She relaxed into the seat as I drove through the streets and sighed. "I can't believe I actually thought my mom would get her head around this and be happy for us."

"Well, she does have a lot to deal with herself," I pointed out. "The pregnancy, and her and Pat. Maybe things aren't great between them and she's lashing out."

I didn't think it was that, but I had to throw some option up in the air so that Chastity didn't think it was her fault.

"Let's not talk about my parents anymore," she said, sighing again. "I want to just go home, have a long shower, eat our food and make love all night long like we used to."

I glanced across at her to make sure she wasn't joking. We were only about five minutes from home and my body was already reacting to her words.

"Make love all night like we used to? Are you sure?"

She twisted in her seat to smile at me. "Oh, yeah. I've been missing you so much this week and my body is definitely back to where it was hunger-wise."

I turned the last corner and sped down the street. "Think we can fit in a session before the food arrives?"

Chastity laughed and checked her phone. "Twenty-two minutes until arrival. What do you think?"

I pulled the car into the parking garage and turned the engine off. "I think we better hurry or hope the Uber guy is late." I hadn't made love to Chastity in so long, I had blue balls just thinking about how good it was going to be.

I grabbed her hand and hurried her to the elevator doors, her delighted giggle ringing in my ears.

Chapter 3

Chastity

Mom was a being a bitch. She always had the capacity, especially if you crossed her, but I'd never really been on the receiving end before. I didn't like to admit it, but I'd still spent my whole life wanting to please her, chasing her approval. And a large part of me still felt like I owed her for all the sacrifices she'd made for me when I was a child.

But that still didn't give her the right to tell me I shouldn't have my baby now. I was fifteen weeks, and it was a bit late to tell me she thought I was making a mistake. Especially when I would never say the same thing to her about her pregnancy. Her baby was a miracle statistically and would be the second chance she wanted with my dad. I could see that, and even though she'd thrown it in my face, I could understand where she was coming from.

That didn't mean I wasn't angry. I was furious. But for tonight, she was no longer my focus.

As soon as we got into the elevator, I grabbed for Axel and kissed him hard, throwing my passion into the kiss and feeling his lust surge against mine like two cresting waves pushing against one another.

He pressed me up against the cold, mirrored wall and I gasped at the contrast of his warmth at my front and the cold at my back.

The doors dinged open, and Axel pulled me out of the elevator and into the apartment. He tugged at my dress, but I was too impatient wait for him to take it off. Instead, I stepped back from him to grab my dress around the waist and pulled it over my head then dropped it to the floor beside me.

Axel's eyes widened as he scanned my changing body, still clad in the nice black underwear I'd bought just for tonight.

When his gaze met mine, lust was written all over his face, from his darkened eyes to his mouth where he licked his lips.

He dove toward me and this time I wrapped my arms around his neck, swept up in the storm of his passion. When he lifted me against his body, I wrapped my legs around his waist, planting kisses on his face and holding on for the ride.

He walked us into the bedroom and there he set me on my feet and pulled his shirt over his head. "Strip off and get on your hands and knees on the edge of the bed."

I was too excited to argue and did as I was told. He got rid of the rest of his clothes and I pushed my panties down my legs and tore my bra off. Then I turned around and knelt on the edge of the bed like he'd asked, going down on my hands so I was in a position that gave him total access to me.

My heart pounded faster than it should as I waited for him, glancing over my shoulder to watch him move behind me.

"I got you a present. Do you want it now?" he asked, running his hand up and down my back.

I shivered at the caress. Not exactly what I'd been expecting him to say. "Ah… do I need it now?"

He grinned, disappeared for a minute and came back with a small, white box. "It's a clit vibe. It's the highest rated one in the shop where I bought it. Want to try it?"

I was pretty sure I was wet enough, but why not? "Sure." The last thing I wanted to do was turn down a gift from him and ruin the mood. Plus, I'd never tried anything like it before.

He handed me a small, pink, silicone tube that looked a bit like a lipstick. He then pressed a button on its base, and I took it from him, the thing vibrating in my hand.

"I'm going to lick you, then enter you," Axel said, staring straight at me. "Set this next to your clit when I'm inside you, all right?"

I nodded, swallowing the groan that rose from his hot words. I loved it when he spoke to me like that.

He knelt down behind me suddenly and used his hands to open my thighs. I turned away, dropping my head to relax my back, then he set his mouth on me.

Sensations pulsed over my flesh as his lips suckled my clit. "Oh! Axel… wow." Then he ran his tongue up my pussy and thrust inside me.

I screamed out, then bucked against his mouth, unable to stop the involuntary jerk of my hips. From that angle, his mouth felt totally different and pressed on my pussy in new and amazing ways.

He stood up too soon and pressed his hard cock against me. "Fuck, you're too hot."

All my focus shifted to the space between my legs where he ran the soft skin of the head of his cock over me. From my swollen, throbbing clit, past my pussy, all the way up to my ass then back again. I moaned as the pleasure washed over me and closed my eyes. "Please fuck me," I whispered.

He pressed the head to my opening and thrust in just a little, making me gasp and ache for more. "Say that again."

I pushed back against him, but he withdrew completely this time. *Shit!* I groaned out in frustration this time. "Please fuck me!"

He grabbed both of my hips and pulled me back, pressing his cock into me again. "Put the vibe on your clit."

I'd totally forgotten about that little thing. "Okay." I rested my weight on my left elbow and extended my right arm under my body to touch the little vibrator to my clit.

I cried out at that first magical touch of vibration against my already sensitized flesh. My clit exploded with pleasure and Axel slid his thick cock straight into me. I came instantly, screaming out at the clenching tightness within my belly.

Axel groaned as he tightened his fingers into my hips. "Damn, you almost made me come right then with you."

I hung my head with a moan and tilted my hips back for him, wanting more.

Axel read my move perfectly, pulling back and piercing me again. I cried out, totally unable to deal with all the pounding into me over and over while the vibe pressed perfectly against my clit, giving me the ultimate in sensation.

The ache inside my belly began to build again and with every stroke of Axel's cock, it pushed me higher and higher. I gasped and groaned, bucking against him.

The harder he thrust, the more I wanted. Both of us raced towards the final climax, pushing harder and faster up the hill.

Just as my clit felt like it couldn't take a single moment more, Axel thrust deep inside of me and called out.

He came, and heat flooded my belly, setting off my final orgasm. I screamed, closing my eyes as wave after wave of sensation rolled over me.

Axel pulled out and collapsed onto the bed beside me, sweaty and flushed. "Oh my God. That was so hot."

I grinned at him. "So hot." It had been perfect, but damn I was even more hungry now. "Do you think the Thai guy dropped the food and ran?"

Axel laughed. "Probably. I'll go check." He jumped up and walked out of the room. The perfect boyfriend.

I rolled onto my back and held up the little vibe so I could press the button and turn it off. "Now that's a great present."

When Axel came back, he was still naked and had bags of Thai in his hands. "Picnic in bed?"

"Oh, absolutely!" That sounded perfect after amazing sex.

I shuffled to the top of the mattress and sat up against the headboard, cupping my belly with my hand. I was getting bigger by the day, and I was loving it.

I couldn't wait to wear those tight tops that showed off my big, swollen stomach.

"Here you go." Axel handed me some cutlery then spread out the takeout containers for us to eat from.

"This is perfection to me," I said, grabbing some noodles and opening the lid of the container. "Just you and me, in our bed, talking, eating. What else could you want?"

I took a bite of the chicken stir fry and groaned. "God, this is good."

We ate quickly, barely talking as we were both so hungry. But after some rice, chicken, noodles and soup, I sat back and sighed. "Thank you for that. It was great."

"You ordered it through your phone, which means you paid for dinner," Axel said with a frown. "I'll transfer some money over."

He reached for his phone, and I swatted at him. "Don't you dare. You paid for dinner tonight and it was my fault we didn't get to eat it. I'm sorry about that."

What a waste it had been. Our delicious meals would have sat there looking so sad and lonely without us.

"Do you think Dad would have eaten our dinner too?" I asked, suddenly imagining my father's expression when he realized we weren't coming back.

Axel, who was still eating his prawn rice noodles, shrugged. "Probably. I've seen him put away three steaks in a sitting."

I sighed and climbed under the blankets. "I wish I didn't have to go back tomorrow. I'd rather just stay here and watch movies and relax."

Knowing Axel would be working for most of the day, made staying a moot point. I didn't want to relax alone.

"Well, I don't have to do much until six-ish. We could go out for brunch, then chill together for the afternoon."

"Seriously?" I asked him, putting my head on the pillow and watching as he lifted the food containers off the bed and slowly closed them up.

"Yes, seriously. I told you I want to slow down and enjoy life, and there's only one way to do that."

He certainly sounded serious. I needed to do some studying, but at the moment, I didn't care about anything other than getting the rest my body craved.

"You're right. We need to get used to spending Sundays together," I announced. "Family days. Brunch and movies."

"And more sex," he added with a sexy grin.

I most certainly wasn't going to argue that.

"Oh, definitely!" I said, then yawned, my tiredness getting to me. "That clit thing was amazing. Thank you for buying it for me."

Axel was an amazing boyfriend. How many guys were confident and secure enough in themselves to buy their girlfriend a sex toy?

"You're welcome," he said, gathering all the containers up in his hands. "Give me a minute to clean up and I'll be back to sleep with you soon."

"Take your time," I whispered, settling into the pillow.

He disappeared into the kitchen, and I closed my eyes. Tomorrow I'd enjoy spending time with Axel, but for now, I needed sleep.

Chapter 4

Axel

Sunday with Chastity was fantastic, and so much more relaxing than I'd expected. We had great sex, then a huge brunch. More hot sex, then watched a movie on the couch in my apartment.

Well, I watched a movie while mentally planning my workday on Monday. Lists. Emails. Meetings.

Chastity watched the first ten minutes of the movie with her head resting on my shoulder and her hand on my leg, then fell asleep.

When the movie finally ended, I turned the TV off and the sound changing seemed to wake her up.

"Oh… I missed the ending." She groaned as she lifted her head off my chest and sat up.

I rolled my shoulder where it had gone numb half an hour ago. I'd been too afraid to wake her, so I'd never moved.

"You missed most of it, sweetheart, but at least you got some rest." I stood up and stretched my back, extending my hand to her to help her to her feet. "How about we order a late lunch? What time is the driver taking you back to school?"

She rubbed her eyes and yawned. "I asked him to come around four pm. What's the time?"

I glanced at my watch. "Ah… about three forty-five."

"Oh, shit." She raced for my bedroom, calling out as she went, "I've gotta pee, then pack, then go."

I walked over to the bedroom and called out to the closed bathroom door, "I can ask him to come back in a couple of hours if you want to go out for dinner before you go."

The extra time for me to work would be helpful of course, but I wanted her to know that we always had flexibility with our drivers.

I paid for the privilege.

She stepped back into the bedroom from the ensuite and started picking up her things. Her cell, her bag, her clothes. "That sounds so lovely, Axel. Thank you. But I really need to get back. Got finals coming up."

She put all her things into a large overnight bag she'd brought, and I grinned at her. She was happy to go back to school, which meant she was content with us overall.

"Okay. Great. What else can I do?" I asked.

She launched herself at me and I swept her up into a hug, pulling her hard into my body.

"Nothing," she squealed. "You've been amazing. Thank you."

I walked her to the elevator and kissed her goodbye, wishing she didn't have to go.

As she was stepping into the lift, she put her hand against the door, stopping them from closing. "Hey, I want you to know how much I appreciate you asking my dad to come work for you. It was really good of you."

I glanced down at the marble floor and ran a hand through my hair. I didn't know why it embarrassed me to have her be grateful for such a thing, but it did.

"I'm doing it for all of us," I told her. "Pat is amazing in his field, and I think he'd be an asset to my company. I can pay him a lot more than he currently makes, which will benefit your mom and him."

I'd happily just transfer a million dollars into his account if it would make his life easier, but Patrick was proud, and I knew he'd prefer to earn it.

She grinned at me, happiness twinkling in her eyes, "I know you're justifying your kindness by saying the decision was made purely on its merits, but I know you're doing it to help him. And my mother. And me."

I smiled at her, grateful for her understanding. "I need someone I trust at the helm with me. And Pat fits the bill."

He was the only man on the planet I truly trusted. He had integrity and a great work ethic. Time would tell if we could be friends, family and work colleagues.

Unfortunately, I'd heard some horror stories about mixing the two, but it was time to step out of my comfort zone. I'd never gotten anywhere by staying inside the box.

"I love you," Chastity chimed as she stepped back into the elevator and let the doors close in front of her.

I held my hand up and said, "I love you too," though I wasn't sure she heard me since the doors closed on my words.

I sighed and glanced around. The apartment was so quiet now. So empty. Exactly how I used to love it.

Not so much anymore I realized, as the silence sank down onto me like a weight around my neck.

I sighed once more and moved into the kitchen, cleaned up, made myself a protein shake and headed for the office.

It was midnight the next time I checked the time. I'd gotten a lot of work done and was prepared for the week, including Patrick's impromptu interview.

THE NEXT DAY, I WAS UP AND GONE BY SIX. I WENT TO THE GYM, HAD breakfast, and was in the office by eight am. My new managers were already in, working away in the conference room Cheryl had allocated for them until we could find the right space to put them all.

I liked having them close by my office, and them being together meant they brainstormed and bounced ideas off each other.

"How are they doing?" I asked Cheryl as I stood by her desk, staring at the trio through the glass windows of the meeting room.

Cheryl gave me a rare smile. "They're doing very well. A little too enthusiastic at times, but I can't fault their work. Or their intent. What are you going to do about them?"

"What do you mean?"

"They need a leader. You and I know that. And you can't do it. You're too busy."

I grinned at my office manager. Always one step ahead. "I have Pat coming in today to meet them. I've offered him the job."

"Patrick Johnson? Your friend?"

"Yes, that's him. And Chastity's father, too."

Cheryl's mouth dropped open, then she snapped it up again. Damn, where was a camera when you needed one? First and probably last chance I'd ever have of capturing a moment when I shocked Cheryl.

"I didn't know that was the connection," she admitted.

I grinned, supressing the laugh that rose. "When we met, we didn't know the connection either. And once we did, it was too late."

And thank God for that. If I'd met Chastity as Pat's daughter, I would never have looked at her as anything more than the daughter of a friend.

"How is her pregnancy going?" Cheryl asked, her tone all business.

"Good," I answered in the same tone. "Fifteen weeks, I think. Baby's healthy. She's healthy."

Another thing I thanked the universe for.

"And college? When does she graduate?" Cheryl asked again.

I glanced at my office manager, who'd never shown more than a professional interest in my personal life before. "A month or two. Not long now."

"Hmmmm. Okay. I'll get back to work and bring Patrick around to you when he arrives."

I stopped myself from responding with a "thanks, boss." Sometimes it truly felt like I worked for Cheryl, not the other way around.

"Thanks."

Cheryl headed off and I went back to work.

At one pm, there was a knock on my office door and Patrick

walked in. "Those three are going to take over this company, Axel. You're in trouble."

I laughed and closed my laptop. "You've been here less than a minute and you've already worked that out?"

"I got here half an hour ago and have just been hanging out with Cheryl and listening in on the three of them. They swap between English, French and some other language I didn't pick up on."

I grinned at him and gestured to the chair in front of me. "You want to sit and chat?"

"Nah. I was thinking we could go out for lunch and talk there. I'm starving and I know you haven't eaten yet."

I stood up and walked around the desk. "Like to take the three vicious babies?"

He shook his head. "No. I already know I want to work with them."

"So, you're in?"

Pat thrust his hands into his pants pockets and nodded his head.

"Don't you want to know the salary? Benefits?"

Patrick laughed and shook his head. "Axel, I know how generous you are. I know I give you hell for your success and your money, and all that shit, but…"

"Hey, look. Don't get soft on me. Here." I turned around and picked up the contract I'd had written up and handed it to him. "This is only the initial offer."

With anyone else, I would never have told them such a thing, but this was Pat.

I half expected him to shove the contract back at me. But he took it, then sat in the chair by my desk.

Okay, so we weren't going straight to lunch.

I sat back on my chair and waited for him to finish reading.

"A car?" he asked.

"Yes." Any car he liked under a hundred thousand.

"Top tier health benefits?"

"Yes. For you and your family." Which would mean that hopefully

Katherine's pregnancy would be covered, though I hadn't checked up on it.

"My salary—"

"Not enough?" I asked. I had room to move. "We could set some bonuses on performance."

Patrick's gaze flicked up to meet mine. "I need two weeks to tie up some loose ends at work, then I can start."

"As easy as that?" I couldn't believe it.

Pat nodded. "Yeah. As easy as that. You got a pen?"

I pushed a pen across the desk towards him and he picked it up and signed on the dotted line.

"Done."

I shook my head. "I can't believe we're finally going to work together."

"Even though we said we never would." Patrick chuckled, pushing the signed document across the desk.

I stood up and walked around the desk, grabbing my jacket. "Lunch to celebrate."

"On you," my buddy said with a grin.

"Of course." And it always would be from now on and my friend couldn't complain.

An hour later we'd drunk a bottle of red wine and eaten a couple of steaks and were sitting in one of our favorite restaurants on a Monday afternoon.

"Don't you have to get back to work?" Pat asked, taking a sip of his water after four glasses of wine.

"Don't you?" I asked him.

He shrugged. "I took the afternoon off."

"Then I will too!" I declared, then ordered us another bottle of red. "I still owe you that birthday meal, and since the other night got shot to hell, we can pretend this is your birthday lunch."

Pat groaned and ran both hands over his face. "Fuck, that was ridiculous. Kaiti is so worried about everything at the moment, and it makes her crazy."

Yeah, makes her a crazy bitch.

"Can I ask you something?"

"Sure." Pat said, taking the bottle of red from the waiter and pouring us both another glass. "At this point in time, I don't think we should have any secrets."

"Why now?" I asked. I'd thought we were pretty solid as friends before.

He glared at me. "Because you got my daughter pregnant, and I saw you two naked in your apartment. I don't think we can get much closer, man."

I burst out laughing, I couldn't help it. "Okay, but I just wanted to know how you're doing about the pregnancy. Katherine's, I mean. You happy about being a dad again?"

"Are you happy about being a dad for the first time ever?"

I stared at him and let my joy spread over my face in a massive grin. "I couldn't be happier. That baby is the best thing that ever happened to me, except for Chastity, of course, and it's not even here yet."

"She's not even here yet," Patrick corrected, then sighed heavily. "I'm going to have a granddaughter. I can't really believe it."

I huffed out a laugh. "I can't believe my daughter is going to be your granddaughter, man. But, hey… stranger things have happened."

"Name one."

I couldn't, and Pat and I spent the rest of the afternoon drinking and laughing.

We sealed our new working relationship with wine and laughs, and it was truly one of the most enjoyable days I'd had in a very long time.

Chapter 5

Chastity

THE NEXT MONTH FLEW BY. I WAS SUPER BUSY AT SCHOOL, AND AXEL was hectic at work. But he drove every weekend to spend time with me or more accurately, he was driven. I liked to joke with him that he was turning into a regular old billionaire now, having a full-time driver, but he just laughed and said it was my fault. I'd told him to delegate some jobs so he could work more effectively, and allegedly, driving was one of them.

My dad and I chatted every other day, and he and Axel were getting on well at work. They were both men who tended to be masters of the understatement, especially when it came to their own accomplishments, but if I had to guess, I'd say they were killing it together.

In fact, it was time I checked on it.

My driver arrived, thanks to Axel's protectiveness now that I was twenty weeks, to drive me to my sonogram in the city. I'd offered to be closer to him so he could make it easily from work.

As we set off, I put my bag on the seat next to me and picked up my phone, calling Axel's office.

A familiar voice answered the phone and I grinned. "Hi, Cheryl, it's Chastity!"

"Hello, young lady. How are you feeling today?"

"Great, actually. A bit nervous about my sonogram, but I'm sure everything will be fine." One hand went to my basketball of a belly as I said the words.

I'd read so many horror stories online about women losing their babies later in pregnancy. I didn't know how I'd cope if I lost her now, especially since I could feel her kicking and shifting, moving around in there.

"I'm sure you will be fine," Cheryl said, in her mothering tone. "And I'll make sure Axel doesn't miss it, even if I have to drive him there myself."

I laughed out loud at the image her words evoked. "I love you, Cheryl. You're awesome."

"Well, you're a good girl, Chastity, and I'm very grateful Axel has found someone like you."

We were silent for a moment, and I enjoyed the glow between us.

I'd never met nor spoken to Axel's mother. By all accounts, she was a cold, horrible woman.

My mom didn't want to talk to me, and for the sake of our health and our babies' health, I'd decided it was best not to try and contact her. Dad kept me up to date with any pertinent info, and I had to assume he did the same with her.

So as far as I was concerned, Cheryl was the only maternal influence Axel or I had at the moment, so it was nice to hear such beautiful words come from her.

"Thank you, Cheryl. I appreciate it."

"So, that said, what can I do for you, young lady?"

I grinned. And there she was. The business manager was back.

"I'd like a report, please."

"A report?"

She sounded confused, so I grinned. "Yes. I want to know how my dad and Axel are getting along. Neither of them will tell me the truth. They only say it's going fine, but I know you'll tell me, Cheryl."

"I'm going to put you on hold for a moment, okay?"

"Of course." Was she running to another room so we could gossip without all her staff listening in?

Within a minute she was back on the line. "Thanks for holding, I had to move from where I was."

"That's no problem, Cheryl." Of course, she had to move. I knew it. She had gossip.

"I'm not sure I should report in on my boss, Chastity."

Yeah, right.

"I don't need specifics, Cheryl. I just want to make sure there isn't going to be some big blow-up. You know, with them being nearly related because of me, best friends, and now work colleagues I've been extremely nervous about how they're getting along, but neither of them will say much about how things are going."

Cheryl laughed softly. "I can tell you that things are going much better than even I anticipated, and I had great hopes for the alliance."

"Really?" I asked, happiness filtering through my chest. "Are they getting along that well?"

Did they have lunch together? Brainstorm ideas? Did Dad have an office next door to Axel's now?

Cheryl chuckled. "Well, they don't spend a lot of time together. Patrick oversees the managers and takes responsibilities off Axel, which leaves him to do more CEO-related tasks, and he ends up walking around and talking to them instead. I'm finding it… funny."

She was finding it funny?

"How is it funny?" She would probably be the only one that found it humorous that Axel was out of his depth.

She huffed out a laugh. "Yes. I don't think he knows what to do with himself some days. The younger managers are doing a fantastic job and your father oversees them well. Teaches them while he's guiding them. I think he'll help Axel take the whole company to the next level, if Axel's ready for it."

I frowned. "Why wouldn't Axel be ready for it?"

He worked harder than anyone else I knew and had achieved so much in his lifetime already.

"I'm not saying he's not, but it would require a lot of time and dedication on his part, and I think his focus has shifted."

"I…" I didn't know what to say. I knew his focus had shifted. He had a life now. A partner and a baby on the way.

"Don't get me wrong, Chastity, I'm glad he's changed priorities and has you. But you should know that his business model has the capacity to double and triple his revenue if it grows the way he's always planned for. And with your father at his side, I think they can do truly amazing things."

I nodded to myself. "Thanks, Cheryl."

It wasn't exactly the report I'd wanted, but she'd given me an honest one, that was for sure.

"I better go," Cheryl said. "Good luck with the scan this afternoon. It's two pm, correct?"

"Yes." And in a rare moment of worry about Axel, I'd actually forgotten about the scan. That's what I needed to focus on. My baby. Our life together. Not the worries that came with dating a billionaire.

Cheryl said goodbye and hung up.

I put my phone down on the seat next to me, deflated. I'd gone into the conversation looking for gossip and something happy to focus on, but instead I felt sad.

Cheryl was saying that Axel and my dad worked brilliantly together. So brilliantly, in fact, they could push past some glass ceiling and go up and onward. But only if I got out of the way.

Was that true? Was that what Axel wanted? To live to work. Or was I being unfair in making him choose?

I didn't know, but I had to talk to him about it.

The car trip took longer than I thought it would, probably because instead of studying, I spent the time worrying. But soon enough, I was in the waiting room filling out another form when Axel walked in.

"Hey, sweetheart," he greeted me, sitting on the chair next to me. "How's your day been?"

He wore an expensive suit and looked powerful. Hot, in fact.

What was the question again? My day? "Oh, fine," I said, loving the way his hand slid straight onto my thigh.

Protective. Possessive.

I reached for his hand to hold, my stomach churning. "Hey, Axel?"

"Yeah?"

How did I ask this nicely? "Am I holding you back?"

He twisted in his chair to stare at me. "What are you talking about?"

"I mean… your business is doing so well, and you and Dad are doing great things, and well, I don't want to be the reason you don't achieve some goals you've set for yourself."

Axel frowned at me. "I'm confused."

And he should be. I'd gone out of my way to make sure he worked less, and now I was having second thoughts?

"I'm sorry, it's just… Are you happy?"

"Of course, I'm happy," he said, squeezing my hand and smiling at me.

"I know, but have I ruined work for you?"

HE SIGHED. "LOOK, WORK IS STRANGE AT THE MOMENT. THE management team has taken so much of my workload, at times I'm not sure what I should be doing."

I grinned at him, needing to make a joke. "Yeah, but you needed four people just to take over some of your work. What does that say about how much you were doing?"

Axel chuckled. "Well, yeah, there's that."

"Chastity?" The receptionist called and I stood up.

It was time. "Come on, Daddy," I said to Axel. "Let's go see our baby."

Axel stood with a grin, and we walked into that small, white room. I lay on my back and lifted my top, and the sonographer smiled at me as she got the lubricant ready.

"This is a longer scan as we're looking at all the anatomy. So… here we go."

She set the probe on my belly, and I looked towards the screen, the black and white lines soon wriggling into the shapes that I knew so well.

"There she is," I whispered and glanced towards Axel.

He was staring at the screen with an intense look on his face.

"You know it's a girl?" the sonographer asked.

"Yes." I grinned. "The blood test said the baby's a girl. Are they ever wrong?"

"Let's just check," the sonographer said, swiping the probe over my belly. "No, they weren't wrong. That's a little girl."

Axel sat down in the chair next to me and grinned. "She's beautiful."

I stared at him, feeling my love grow bigger and stronger. "She is."

"So, there's the head. Let's just measure the circumference."

The sonographer went on the measure the whole baby, noting that she was healthy and well. No anomalies, measuring exactly to term.

When we left, I was filled with happiness and clutching more pictures for my wall.

"I'm so glad you were here to see her," I told Axel as we walked outside into the fresh air. "Do you want some of the pictures?"

He nodded. "Yes. Can I have the hand one?"

I laughed at him. "Of course!"

It was my favorite too, but I wasn't going to stop him for taking the one he wanted. I sorted through the little stack of printouts and handed it to him. "There's something special about her little hands, isn't there?"

He took the picture, then nodded. "Yes. She's perfect."

Then he glanced back at me. "Are you going to stick around? Have dinner together?"

I put my hand on his arm and sighed. "I'd love to. Do you have time?"

"Of course, I do. We could go back to the apartment and spend a couple of hours in bed?"

My lower belly clenched at the suggestion in his voice. "Oh, yes, please."

He wrapped his hands around my waist and drew me into him. I went with him, wanting to be as close to his warmth as possible, sliding my hands around his neck and pulling him down to me for a kiss.

An afternoon of sex and food sounded like heaven to me.

Chapter 6

Axel

I stood in the main area of my main business floor—a sea of low walled cubicles—and glanced around the office filled with people, marveling at the amount of work being done. Patrick was in the conference room yelling at someone, and everywhere I looked, people were on the phone, staring at computers or rushing to another meeting.

"Surveying your kingdom?" Cheryl asked deadpan as she walked up to stand beside me.

"Well, yeah." I assumed she was joking, of course. But in a way, I suppose I was looking at what I'd created. What my business sustained. Lots of people with jobs, supporting themselves and possibly families. That was an achievement. And I what I liked about it the most was the fact I'd built it up from nothing. My parents hadn't given me squat. "Can you believe it was just you and me in the beginning?"

Cheryl rolled her eyes. "I had to bring coffee mugs from home because there was no money for extras."

A laugh burst out of me at the thought. "Yeah, I remember that."

Twenty years had changed many of things, but not my appreciation for Cheryl. I stared at her as she glanced around, checking on the staff like a mother hen watching over her chicks.

Perhaps it was time to show my appreciation in a bigger way that a simple "thank you."

"I was wanting to talk to you, actually. Do you have time now, Cheryl?"

Cheryl met my gaze as though assessing my intent, then nodded once. "Yes, I've got five minutes."

I chuckled to myself as I walked back to my office, Cheryl trailing behind me. She had five minutes to spare me, did she? Better not keep her then.

I walked over to my desk, turned around, and leaned against the edge. This wasn't a meeting, and I didn't need to sit in my executive chair. "I won't keep you long, but I wanted to tell you that I appreciate everything you've done for me. For this company."

Cheryl narrowed her eyes at me. "Why does it sound like you're about to fire me?"

"Oh God, no!" I cried, shaking my head. "You couldn't be more wrong."

She stood patiently, and I realized she was waiting for me to continue. But the problem was, I didn't have anything actually planned. Time to think on my feet.

"Well, I want to know how I can reward your loyalty and hard work, Cheryl. A yearly bonus, perhaps? A raise? Tell me what you want and it's yours."

I already paid Cheryl well, but nowhere near what I paid my Ivy League managers, which didn't make sense when I thought about it. Without her, this place probably wouldn't exist.

Cheryl shook her head at me. "I'm not really comfortable talking about raises and such, Mr. Patterson. You've always been very generous with my yearly increments."

I stood up from the desk I leaned on and stared at the woman before me. "Can I ask you about your retirement plans, Cheryl? How many years do I have you for, before you leave me?"

Cheryl smiled, though it was tight. "Well, my youngest is still in college, and the bills for that are still coming in. So, I'm hoping another ten years or so."

Perfect. "You have two children, correct?"

We didn't talk about a lot of personal stuff, Cheryl and I, but I'd heard enough to know she was married with two sons.

"Yes. Michael is twenty-seven and Tommy is twenty-one."

"What's the balance of his tuition fees and boarding?"

Cheryl didn't answer, but her eyes went wide as though she were already a step ahead and on to my plan.

I just crossed my arms over my chest and smiled at her. "I can guess, if you want me to."

She swallowed hard, her throat working. "It's close to a hundred thousand, I believe. But we're happy to do it, of course. Anything to help the boys succeed."

The perfect mother. Something I'd never had.

I walked around my desk and pulled out my check book from my top drawer. "Cheryl, without you, I would never have made it past the first year. Without you, I would never have found Taylor or hired Patrick."

I sat down in the chair and grabbed a pen. "You have been a mentor to me in many ways, so please take this as a bonus for all your hard work." I wrote out a check for a hundred grand, tore it off, then got up again and walked over to her. "With my heartfelt thanks."

I held it out, and Cheryl's bottom lip quivered. "Mr. Patterson, I couldn't possibly"

"You can, and you will. Or I'll just send it over to your house in cash. Unless you'd prefer that?"

"No... I..." Her gaze darted from the paper to me and back again. She seemed to finally realize I was serious and her hand shook as she reached for the check and put her fingers on the paper. "Axel, I don't know what to say."

Cheryl rarely used my first name, and it tugged at my heart when she did.

"Just don't leave me yet. Not until I figure out what I'm going to do next. With work and Chastity. Everything."

Cheryl swiped at the tear that rolled down her cheek, then she nodded. "No. We still have a lot to do before I can retire."

I leaned back on my desk and smiled at the woman who was still standing in the middle of my office, nearly speechless.

"That's all I needed to tell you, Cheryl. If you want to go to the bank before they close, maybe leave early today?"

She nodded slowly, her lip doing that quivering thing like she was about to cry, then she turned on the ball of her foot and walked out without saying another word.

I sat and relaxed back into my chair and sighed. That had been well overdue.

And felt great.

I reached for my mouse and began scrolling through emails. I needed a bigger fish, a larger project. Patrick had the managers under control, and the manager trio had most of my work covered. I needed more.

MORE CAME THE WEEK CHASTITY GRADUATED. SHE GOT THROUGH HER exams, packed her stuff and drove back to the city in her car.

The door opened and she called out, "I'm here!"

I jumped at the sound, then grinned. I was going to have to get used to that since she was moving in.

I got up from my computer and walked out into the living room. "Welcome home."

Chastity dropped her bag on the floor and stretched her arms out wide. "To my million-dollar apartment? Ha."

She rubbed her belly and glanced around.

More like 5 million, but I wasn't going to correct her.

"How's my baby?" I asked, walking up and putting my hands on either side of Chastity's belly the way she liked.

I cupped the solid flesh that was almost like she'd stuck a basketball under her t-shirt.

"She's wonderful," Chastity answered, then leaned forward and kissed me, tasting of sweetness and love.

I picked up her one bag. "Should I call the concierge to get your other bags from the car?"

"Yeah, that would be great. Thanks."

I made the call and soon enough, Chastity's bags were piled up in my bedroom and she was sitting on the couch, rubbing her stomach.

We needed to work out where she was going to put everything. My bedroom closet was full.

I glanced at the time. It was only three pm. "We've got a few hours before dinner. Are you okay if I keep working?"

Should I even ask that in my home? Our home? What was the protocol here?

Chastity answered for me. She just stood up, cupped my face and kissed me quickly. "Do whatever you need to do. I'm going to have a quick nap because my feet are killing me. Shower, unpack maybe. See you in a few hours."

She headed off towards the bedroom, a hand on the small of her back.

I sighed. I wouldn't mind having a lie down either, but when was the last time I had a nap in the afternoon?

I turned towards the study, the email I was halfway through calling my name.

Then I heard Chastity groan and sigh and I stopped.

"Screw it."

I unbuttoned my shirt and walked into the bedroom where Chastity was pulling back the covers, wearing panties and a thin tank top.

"Oh, are you joining me?"

I unzipped my pants and slid them off. "Yes, I think I will."

Chastity laughed happily as she slid into bed, surrounded by pillows, one between her legs and one in front of her.

"You've built yourself a bit of a pillow wall," I remarked, sliding onto the mattress.

She made a contented noise. "Hmm... Not behind me, though."

I cuddled in behind her, sliding a hand over her hip and closing my eyes. "I've missed you." Especially at night. Sleeping without her was impossible. I always slipped back into bad habits, getting only three or four hours most nights.

"I hope so, because you're not getting rid of me now."

I kissed her neck and whispered, "Thank God for that."

She fell asleep almost immediately. I didn't think I would. Sleeping during the day had never been my thing.

Sleeping, full stop, had never been my thing. But sleep, I did. And when I woke up, Chastity was still there, my baby kicking away beneath my palm.

"Oh, wow, she's moving," I said, loving the feel of the shift and push against my hand.

Chastity groaned, rolling onto her back. "Sorry, have to move. My hips are killing me."

I ran my hand over her bump, marveling at the movement going on. "This is incredible."

"Yeah, it is." Chastity smiled, lying happily in my arms. "What are we doing for dinner?"

It was Saturday night and there were a hundred places we could go. "We could go out if you're up for it. Japanese? Italian?"

"I'd love to go out and celebrate a little. We didn't get to do anything after my graduation."

"I'm sorry, sweetheart. I had to fly to France, and well…"

I hadn't gone to graduation for several reasons, but mostly because I wanted Chastity to enjoy it and not worry about what sort of fight her mom and I were going to get into.

Chastity and her mother still weren't really talking, but Katherine had gone to the ceremony, mostly because Patrick had dragged her there.

"You wanted to let my parents have the moment, I get it. I just missed you. I wanted you to be proud of me too."

Love filled my chest. "I *am* proud of you. Very proud of you. I would have completely understood you deciding to just quit school to have the baby, but here you are, a college graduate."

"And five months pregnant," she said with glee, rubbing her hands over her belly again.

"Yes, you are." I pressed my lips to her belly, then rolled out of bed. "Let's go then. Dinner."

"Shower first," she said, getting up slowly. "Are you going to join me?" She looked over her shoulder with a sultry expression I'd missed.

Heat flooded my groin and my cock hardened. "Hell, yeah."

I followed her into the bathroom where she shrugged off her tank and panties, shaking her ass for me.

"How are you going to be most comfortable?" I asked, jumping straight to it. "From behind?"

She turned the water on and wiggled her ass again. "Is that vibe thing waterproof?"

"Yes." I walked out of the bathroom and grabbed the clit vibe and some lube from the nightstand. I didn't want to hurt her, and her body was changing every day.

When I walked back in the room, my cock was throbbing. I grabbed some lube and worked my shaft, loving the way she stared at me as I did it.

"Damn, I've missed you." I told her. "Have you missed me?"

She nodded, the water cascading over her rounded body. "Yes."

"Have you missed my cock in your pussy?"

She groaned and cupped her hands around her breasts, squeezing her darkened nipples. "Oh my God, yes."

I walked forward and grabbed her, kissing her hard. Her arms came around my body, then moved down to my cock, squeezing the head.

I turned her away from me, deciding to test out a theory I had. She liked me talking dirty to her, or at least telling her what I wanted to do to her. She always flushed pink when I did.

So I said, "Put your hands on the wall and stick your ass back if you want me to fuck you."

She gasped and did exactly as I'd ordered. Her fingers splayed over the grey tiles, and she bent forward, sticking her ass back and opening her legs for me.

I pressed the button on the clit vibe and slid it around her hip. "Use this. Get yourself nice and ready for me."

"Oh. I'm ready." She gasped, pressing the vibe to her clit. She wiggled her hips, tempting me.

I put my hands on her thighs and rubbed my cock between her spread legs, over her lips, driving us both crazy.

"Tell me what you want."

"You." She panted, pressing back.

I would have laughed if I hadn't been so horny. "Do you like me telling you how much I want to fuck you?"

There was a soft pause, then she groaned. "Yes."

Then I was right, and I'd make sure I told her a lot more often. "We're going to discuss that later, what you want me to say to you. But for now, I want your pussy to squeeze me so tightly I come in you."

"Yes. Oh, yes, please." She panted, hanging her head forward.

I slid my hand between her legs, thrusting a finger deep into her pussy, testing how ready she was for me.

She moaned and wriggled on my finger, so I withdrew it and replaced it with my cock, thrusting deeply.

"Oh, God, yes. My beautiful girl," I groaned out, rocking into her perfect heat again and again.

She came once, squeezing my cock hard.

"Oh God…" I closed my eyes and held tight to my control, fucking her through the ripples and up that mountain again. Deep and hard and fast, until we were both screaming and hot water ran over our satisfied bodies.

Chapter 7

Chastity

Moving in with Axel was strange but so natural at the same time. Asking him for space to be cleared in the closet took some time, but soon enough he'd sorted out what he needed on a daily basis, and we split the walk-in space. I moved his extra items to the closet in the spare bedroom.

"Maybe we should have his and hers closets at the new house," he'd joked, which inspired me to go on a house search.

I was heading towards six months pregnant, and now that school was finished, I had nothing to fill my time with except my health and planning for the future.

Axel left for work around seven am and often didn't get home until dinner time.

One night he'd asked me how my day was, and I begrudgingly admitted, "I'm bored."

He stared at me like he'd never heard the word before. "Ah… sorry. You'll need to define that better for me."

I sighed and dropped my fork. "I don't know what to do all day while you're at work. I feel like I need a job or something."

Axel's mouth opened and shut, then he finally said, "But you're six months pregnant."

I ran my hands through my hair, then pulled it up into a bun on top of my head. "I've been looking at houses for us, and I found one I really like. It's got lots of character, and a great location. Close to your work and my parents."

Mom and I occasionally texted each other, but we really needed to have it out properly.

She'd need my support when her baby came, and I certainly needed her now.

"That's fantastic. When can we see it?" Axel asked.

I jumped up from the table. "I'll get my laptop and show you now."

I heard his chuckle as I tried to race to the bedroom, though running while waddling wasn't the most normal thing.

When I returned, he'd cleared the table and I sat down to search out what I'd found. "I'm not sure if this is the sort of thing you're going to like. It's not super modern and it needs a little work, but I'd really like the project. I could paint the baby's room, and maybe hire contractors and oversee updates."

I'd never done anything like it before but I was sure with Axel's connections and money, I could learn.

"Show me," Axel said, so I did.

"It's four bedrooms, with a study as well," I told him, showing him the layout of the house. "The lot is huge for the area, but the house needs new carpets, maybe a new kitchen."

"On Patterson Drive?" Axel asked, his lips quirking up at the joke. "Is that going to be weird, or is it meant to be?"

I grinned up at him. "I think it's meant to be."

"Can I have a quick look?" he asked, gesturing to the laptop.

"Of course." I pushed the computer at him and watched as he clicked and scrolled and scanned what I'd found.

"I've looked at hundreds of listings," I told him, feeling the need to fill the silence with my chatter. "From inner-city apartments to huge blocks out of town."

"And this was your favorite?" he asked, still staring at the computer.

"Well, yes. There are more finished, more expensive properties, of course." Though this one was still insanely expensive. I'd had a heart attack the prices over the first few days, but after a chat with Cheryl that Axel didn't know about, she'd told me not to even look at the price and just choose the house that my heart wanted.

After all, it was Axel's money. He was the one who should say if it was too expensive or not, and that was a direct quote from Cheryl.

"I like it," Axel finally said. "I've always wanted a pool in my family home, so we'll need to see if there's room for one in the backyard."

"Oh, yeah, that would be amazing. I just thought with the house being so expensive, we'd need to wait to do those sorts of improvements."

Axel leaned forward and kissed me. "We don't have to wait."

I threw my arms around his neck and burrowed my head into his shoulder, tears filling my eyes.

"Hey, are you okay?"

He pulled back, so I had to look down and blink away the tears. "Yeah, I'm fine. It's just the hormones," I admitted, fanning my face with my hands. "I'm too emotional lately."

He grinned at me then kissed me again. "You're perfect. Now, do you want me to call the real estate agent?"

"Could you?" I asked, knowing Axel would do a much better job than me. "You know your way around that stuff."

He nodded. "Give me ten minutes."

He took out his cell phone, took the number of the real estate agent off the screen, and walked away to the office.

I sat on the chair, wanting to squeal but holding it in. We were going to buy a house to raise our daughter in, together. It was unbelievable.

Axel was chatting to someone on the phone, so to keep busy, I quickly rinsed the dishes and loaded the dishwasher. He was back soon after.

"Well, I have some good news," he said with a grin.

"Tell me."

"The house is empty and the owners are wanting a quick sale, so we'll be able to negotiate a lower price. So once we see it and it passes inspection, we may be able to get going on the renovations sooner than expected."

"Before the baby's born?" I asked, this time my voice rising to the squeak I'd been afraid to hit.

He grinned at me. "Yes."

I launched myself at him, hugging him tightly, even though my baby bump made it awkward. "I was afraid that would never happen," I admitted. "That we'd wait too long and then have to move with an infant."

And that sounded like an absolute nightmare to me. Especially if I ended up with a C-section or something that required major rest time afterwards.

Axel pulled back and said, "We haven't seen it yet but if there's any structural damage, then we'll have to move on to something safer. Don't get your hopes up too high, okay?"

I nodded but clapped my hands and he sighed. "They're high already, aren't they?"

I nodded. I'd already driven past the house and planned out all the flowers I'd plant in the front yard. The swing on the porch.

"When can we go see the inside?"

"Tomorrow, around lunchtime. I'll clear my schedule from noon to one."

I hugged him again. "Oh, thank you, thank you."

He kissed my forehead and sighed. "Just be careful not to fall in love with it too quickly. I've been bitten by that bug before, only to find out it's not the right one."

"Okay, I'll try," I reassured him, and he walked off for a shower, shaking his head.

It was too late though, I was totally in love with the place. And I was going to be heartbroken if I found it my dream home wasn't the dream at all.

∼

THE NEXT DAY I DROVE TO THE HOUSE IN MY LITTLE CAR, TALKING TO the baby the whole way. "Your room is the one behind ours. I'll be able to run in and help you anytime you need me. And there's a park down the street, and a massive backyard. Although, Daddy wants a pool, so the backyard might end up pretty small. But then we'll have a pool, so, either way, it's awesome."

I knew I probably sounded insane, but it was how things were with me now.

My whole world was centered around the baby who made my back ache and my belly bulge and my hormones a mess.

She was everything. And I couldn't wait to meet her.

I arrived early and parked down the street a little way so I could check out the neighbors. The blocks were all large, relatively new houses. It was zoned for residential homes and no apartment buildings. And those homes were grand houses, which meant they'd all be well taken care of.

When twelve o'clock struck, a blonde woman parked in the driveway and hustled up to the front door wearing a short skirt and jacket.

I wasn't sure I should approach her. There was something about her demeanor I didn't like. But I was sure Axel would handle her.

I checked my phone and there was a text from Axel.

Two mins away. Just caught a red light.

I smiled as I put my cell phone away. Ever since the debacle around the twelve-week scan, Axel had been extremely thoughtful about messaging me when he was late.

So, I waited. I wasn't going in by myself.

Then the black sports car pulled up and I walked over, grinning as Axel hopped out of the driver's seat.

"Drove yourself for once?"

He laughed. "I wanted to see how far it was from the office."

"And?" I asked.

He grinned. "Twelve minutes."

"Brilliant," I said as he grabbed hold of my hand and started walking towards the front door.

"Great street," he remarked. "Front lawn needs some work, and a new fence."

"Yeah, a higher one, preferably," I agreed. "So, I can bring her around the front and not worry she'll run on the street."

Axel smiled at me. "Are we going to name her yet?"

I shook my head. "No. Not yet, please. I feel… I don't know. It seems like bad luck to name her before she arrives."

Axel sighed. "No problem. But maybe we can discuss options."

"Okay," I agreed. "We can do that." I already had a list of my top ten.

Axel rang the doorbell, and we could hear the rushing of heels clattering on the floor to the door to open it. "Axel Patterson?" the blonde asked, her eyes set on Axel's handsome face and her bright smile firmly in place.

"Yes, and this is my partner, Chastity," he said, gesturing to me.

The blonde's eyes fell on me, and I saw a shift in her face when her gaze fell on my belly.

I rubbed it for good measure. "I'm due in October and we're looking for a family home."

"Oh, well yes! This home is perfect then. Come on in," she said, jumping straight back into professional mode.

"The owners are very motivated to sell and can do a quick closing. The house has seen better days, but the position is incredible."

"You go with her, I'm going to look around," I told Axel, dislodging my hand from his grip while the blonde went off on her own tour.

Axel grinned at me. "Okay."

I walked into the first room, the one I'd already planned to use as Axel's office. It was the smallest, and now that I saw it in person, it was perfect. Great light, and no built-in closet.

I worked my way through the house, noting the need for new paint, new carpets, even a new kitchen and bathrooms long-term.

But the space was incredible. It was twice as big as Axel's apartment, and three times as big as my mom's house.

We would have so much freedom here to work, to live, to play.

"Shall we check out the backyard, beautiful?" Axel asked as I joined the other two in the huge living room.

"Yes, please."

Axel turned towards the blonde. "Can you call your office now and ask about that home inspection? I want to speak to Chastity for a minute."

"Of course, sir," she said, and bustled off.

"Thank you," I said. "She's a bit full on for me."

Axel shrugged. "Most real estate agents are like that. I'm used to it."

He opened the French doors and we walked into the backyard. "So… what do you think?"

I glanced around at the huge, open space. Lots of grass, a garden shed and a huge oak tree right in the middle of the backyard.

"I think this is the best backyard I've ever seen for child to grow up."

Axel stepped behind me and put his arms around my waist. "Good job keeping your enthusiasm in check in front of the agent, but what do you think about the house?"

I closed my eyes and put my head back against him. "I love it."

He kissed my hair. "I do too."

I twisted around in his arms. "What does that mean?"

My heart was beating a little too fast, and although I was afraid for the answer to come, I was also so excited I could barely breathe.

Axel leaned forward and rubbed his nose with mine. "It means that assuming it passes several different inspections, we'll buy it and move in as soon as possible."

"You mean it?" I whispered, already envisioning the baby's room in a kaleidoscope of pink. With a rocking horse, antique crib and rocking chair.

"Of course, I do," he said, kissing me softly. "But let's find out where we stand structure-wise before we make an offer, okay?"

"Okay." I agreed and crossed all my fingers and all my toes.

This was the right house. I could just feel it.

Chapter 8

Chastity

IT WAS A TENSE WEEK WHILE WE WAITED ON THE PEST AND STRUCTURAL inspections, and Axel got quotes for a pool and renovations to the kitchen.

I was sitting on the couch with my swollen feet up when he arrived home early.

"Chastity!" he called out, his voice loud and happy as it echoed through the living room.

I glanced at the time on my cell phone. It was barely five pm.

"I'm here!" I called back. "Just reading." A pregnancy and birth book, as usual.

He walked into the room, grinning from ear to ear.

I swung my legs off the couch and stood up. "Everything okay?" It certainly looked like it, but he wasn't saying anything, so it felt natural to ask.

He schooled his features into a calmer expression, then nodded. "Yes. Everything is great."

My breath caught in my throat. "Did you get news about the house?"

"I did. Everything passed inspection, I put an offer in, and they accepted."

I stared at him, speechless. Did that mean what I thought it meant? "What does that…"

"It means the house is ours."

My hands flew to my mouth as I gasped, shocked.

Axel continued, "We've agreed to a thirty-day settlement, and because the house is vacant, they've also agreed to us going over to get measurements and quotes so the renovations can start as soon as we take possession."

I squealed and rushed forward, hugging him tightly, tears filling my eyes. "I can't believe it." He'd bought us a house for our family to grow in. It was beyond my wildest dreams.

Axel held me tightly against him as he heaved a sigh of relief. "You and me both. I was really worried I was going to have to tell you it failed inspection, and I knew you had your heart set on it."

I laughed as I pulled back, wiping away the tears and reaching for a tissue to blow my nose. "Yeah, I tried not to get attached to it, but I fell in love with that house so quickly."

"It's going to be a change. No concierge. No elevator," Axel said, glancing around at his apartment.

It would be a change for him, but for me, I couldn't wait to get my feet back on solid ground. Plant a tree. Stand with my feet in the grass in my own backyard.

"It's going to be amazing, Axel. I don't know how to thank you."

He smiled as he knelt down in front of me and kissed the baby bump. "I just want you two to be happy. That's all that's important to me."

I lifted my left hand and ran my fingers through his thick hair, staring down at his adored face. "Thank you."

He got to his feet again and started chatting about dinner plans.

I tried to nod and talk, but all I could think about was the house. I got my laptop out and stared at the photos for the hundredth time. The floorplan, the yard.

"Can I tell you what I'm think of for the house? You know, which bedrooms for what use."

Axel chuckled as he opened a bottle of sparkling water. "Please do. Tell me what you're thinking."

I told him which room I wanted for the nursery, and how I wanted to decorate it. I went on to describe every room and Axel hummed and laughed and smiled.

He was listening to me, and I felt heard and loved. It was one of the most fun and happy nights I'd ever had.

Now, if only I could sort out the issues I was having with my mother.

THE NEXT THIRTY DAYS PASSED IN A WHIRLWIND. I WAS ALMOST THIRTY weeks pregnant, and I'd spent the month with architects, designers, and contractors.

The amount of money Axel was throwing at this project was dizzying, but I tried not to focus on it.

My weight was down, and my energy was zapped, but there was only one way forward, and that was to keep working.

I walked into the real estate office to pick up the keys from the blonde who'd sold us the house. Axel and the previous owners had signed all the papers this morning, but Axel had organised for me to pick up the keys.

Her smile as always, was a fake bright, and the baby kicked me hard.

"Ow, baby girl. Relax." I rubbed the spot where she'd kicked me and thanked the blonde.

"Good luck with the new house," she said. "You'll all be very happy there."

"We will," I said with pride, sticking my nose in the air. "Axel's already planned out everything we need for renovations, so I'm very lucky."

"You are," the blonde snapped with a tightness in her voice I didn't understand. "Not all of us can get pregnant to billionaires."

I stared at her, shocked by the words. So, she knew who Axel was, did she?

I could have justified my pregnancy, told her Axel had happily started our family earlier than expected, and loved me more than anything.

But I didn't.

I'd had enough of her crap. "Well, not all of us are massive bitches, so it takes all sorts, doesn't it?" And I walked out of the real estate office with my head held high.

Axel and I knew the truth about our relationship, and I wasn't justifying it to anyone else.

I walked out into the sunshine and Harry, my driver, held open the car door. "To the new house?"

I grinned at him and got into the car, my belly now so large it was difficult to sit behind the wheel myself. "Yes, please, Harry."

He shut the door and we arrived at the new house within five minutes. I'd been there many times over the past month, but never as the owner.

I got out of the car and walked up the sidewalk, glancing around at the huge front yard and fence that would soon be torn down.

So much work still to do, but we'd move in soon, hopefully within the month.

AND THAT WAS EXACTLY WHAT WE DID. BETWEEN AXEL AND ME, WE managed to get the house ready for move-in. We scheduled painters, had the kitchen gutted and remodeled, and all the furniture delivered.

I didn't really like handing off the job of decorating the baby's room to anyone else, but with my blood pressure getting higher and my energy rather low, I ended up finding a compromise.

I located a decorator who hand painted the baby's room and let me watch and chat, being as much a part of it as possible. I still hadn't been able to sort things out with my mom, but it was becoming clear that I needed her, and I was sad she was missing all of this.

Although my dad was always around, at the apartment or on the phone, I wanted my mom.

The day we moved into the new house, I called her.

"Chastity, hello," she greeted as she answered the phone. She didn't sound surprised to hear from me, but she didn't exactly sound excited, either.

"Hey, Mom. How are you doing?"

"I'm fine," she said, but didn't ask about me.

"That's great. Dad said you finished work up early to rest. How's that going?"

Mom's blood pressure had been so high, her doctor put her on bed rest for a month. She was now well enough to go about her normal life if she was careful, but there was no returning to work.

"It's tedious," Mom said then sighed. "Did you take possession of the new house yet?"

My mouth dropped open, shocked. Then I realized that she would know everything Dad did.

"Yeah, we closed a month ago, and its finally ready to move in. I was wondering if you wanted to come over and see it?"

I held my breath as I waited.

Would my mother want to see the sort of house Axel had bought for me?

"I'd like that," she said finally. "What time suits you?"

I glanced around the empty room. "Anytime today, if you want. Axel won't be home until dinnertime. Do you want me to send a car around to pick you up?"

There was a pause.

I knew Mom wasn't supposed to drive herself. She was over thirty weeks, and I was close to thirty-four weeks now. I hadn't seen her in person since my graduation. We'd both look quite different now than we did then.

"Yes. That would be good."

"Okay, great. His name is Harry and I'll call him now. He'll probably be around soon."

She hung up and a thrill of excitement shot through me. I was going to see my mom and show her our new house. A home I was so proud of. A house that in the past would have only been something I would have seen in a magazine.

I called Harry and he said he could pick my mother up in half an hour. Axel had hired him to be our full-time driver the past few months. It seemed overly excessive to have someone on call just to drive Axel and me around, especially when we had our own vehicles. But at times like this, I was grateful for Axel's protective streak.

I raced around the house for the next forty-five minutes. Well, raced is probably an exaggeration, but I changed clothes, brushed my hair and tidied up, wanting to make a good impression.

I put some healthy snacks out on the new granite kitchen island and waited with bated breath for her to arrive.

When my phone rang and it was my father, I jumped on answering it.

"Hey, Dad!"

"Hey, sweetie. Ah… have you invited your mom over for a chat?"

I rolled my eyes. "Obviously she already told you, so what's wrong?"

He wouldn't have called me just to wish me luck.

"Well, I just want to warn you that she hasn't been in the best of moods lately. She might bite your head off over the smallest thing, so please be careful."

I rubbed my hand over my wiggly little girl and sighed. "So, are you… what are you saying exactly, Dad? That I shouldn't have invited her over?"

"No. I'm glad you did. She's been harassing me for months for photos and details of you and your life. Now she can see for herself."

I put a hand on my hip. "If she wanted to see me or our house, why didn't she just ask."

"You know why, Chastity."

I sighed and stared down at my swollen feet. "She's missed my whole pregnancy, Dad."

"I know. And you're missing hers."

His words just hung in the air for far too long, then the doorbell rang through the house.

I twisted around and stared down the long hallway to the large doorway. "I think she's here."

"Okay. Well, just be careful, Chastity. You're both the most important people in the world to me, and I don't want either of you hurt or upset."

"I'll try not to upset her, Dad, but I'm a bit sick of dancing around her. I feel like I've been doing it my whole life."

He sighed. "Yeah, I understand that. And any other time, I'd tell you to just go for it, hash it out with her. But right now, well… you'll see. She's not her normal self."

"Okay, Dad. Better go. Love you."

The doorbell chimed again, and I sighed. Okay, so I had to be on my best behavior, even though everything inside of me considered our time apart my mother's fault.

Come on, Chastity. You're about to be a mother. You can do this.

I walked towards my front door and opened the next chapter of my life.

Chapter 9

Chastity

I OPENED THE DOOR, AND MY MOM WAS STANDING ON THE OTHER SIDE, on my porch.

"Hi, Mom."

My heart ached at the sight of her. She was pale and gaunt. Her eyes had dark circles underneath and she wore way too much makeup.

"This is a nice area," she said casually, glancing around. "You were lucky to be able to buy on this street."

"We were," I agreed. "Very lucky."

Lucky that it came on the market, lucky I found it, and lucky Axel had the money to purchase it.

"Come in," I said, standing back and beckoning her inside. "We only moved in officially a few days ago, so we're not quite unpacked yet."

I didn't know why I was making excuses for the house, it was a piece of art. The interior designers had done a great job.

Mom walked in, slowly, moving carefully.

"Are you okay, Mom?"

"Yes. I'm fine," she answered, though I could tell by the gingerly way she moved, she was in pain.

"Do you want the tour?" I asked.

"Sure," she said. "Where can I leave my bag?"

"Oh, let's go straight to the kitchen and you can put it down there."

I directed her into the huge open kitchen and dining space. She walked in and stood near the granite island, staring at the room in something akin to wonder.

"This is—" She coughed to clear her throat. "—beautiful, Chastity."

"Thanks, Mom," I said, surprised by the compliment already out of her mouth. "The house was in need of a bit of love when we bought it. Everything was a little sad. The walls, the kitchen, the carpets. Everything needed to be replaced."

"You're lucky Axel can afford to do everything all at once."

I bristled at the first shot then smoothed myself. It was true. We were. "Yeah, I know. I can't believe this is our first house, though it could be our last, too. I can't imagine moving."

My mother wandered over to the windows that looked out over the huge backyard. "You haven't done much in the way of landscaping yet."

"No. Axel wants to put in a pool."

She twisted around to look at me. "Aren't you a spoiled one?"

I put a fake smile on my face and calmly asked her, "Are you jealous?"

She crossed her arms over her chest, making her huge belly more prominent beneath the flowing black dress she wore. "Why would I be jealous?"

"You shouldn't be." I told her. "But I can see it in your face. So, you tell me, Mom, why would you be jealous? I know you had it tough, but your life is great now. You have Dad, and a new baby on the way."

She turned away, facing out towards the backyard once more.

When she didn't respond, I walked closer to her and reached out, but I didn't touch her. Too much had passed between us over the last six months, and I wasn't quite ready to just sweep it all under the rug.

In fact, I thought we needed to put it on the table, once and for all.

"You need to tell me, Mom. What's the real problem? Is it Axel? You hate him I suppose because he's rich and too old for me."

She didn't even turn to look at me, just rubbed her belly in slow circles and said, "I don't hate Axel."

I crossed my arms over my chest. "Good. Because he's wonderful to me and makes me very happy."

My mother didn't say anything, so I pushed on. "Okay, so it's not Axel. It must be that you still think I've ruined my life by getting pregnant. That I've thrown away my future because I'm not continuing on to chiropractic school."

She turned around to me slowly, and her eyes were red. "I know you haven't ruined your future, Chastity. Axel will look after you no matter what happens between you, and that sort of financial security is something I never had raising you."

I sighed and let my arms drop to my sides. "I know that, Mom. But I didn't get pregnant on purpose, and I didn't choose Axel because he's rich."

"I know."

"Then what did I do wrong?" I burst out. "You've barely spoken to me for six months and now that you're here, you still won't talk to me."

Mom swayed on her feet, and I rushed forward, grabbing her arm. "Are you okay?"

She nodded, but I could see the sweat on her brow.

"Quick. Let's get you to sit down." I led my mother to the couch and made sure she was sitting down with her feet up before I left her to get something to drink. "What would you like? Cold water? Orange juice?"

"Juice would be nice," she said, though her voice was barely loud enough to hear.

I poured both of us a drink and rushed back to the couch. "What's going on with you, Mom?"

I sat on the couch opposite her, wincing at the pinch in my hip and trying to find a comfortable spot for the baby and me.

"Lots of things are wrong with me." She sighed heavily. "I'm forty-three and having my second baby. The hospital staff treats me like I'm some sort of… oddball, because I dared to get pregnant naturally at my age."

I grinned at her. "Yeah, I suppose most of the women who get pregnant in their forties are through IVF."

She nodded, then took a sip of her juice. "I have high blood pressure and they're pretty sure I'll get pre-eclampsia, which means they'll have to deliver the baby via c-section as soon as it gets too dangerous for both of us."

I gasped, my breath catching in my throat. How horrible. "Oh, Mom, that's terrible. How are you feeling about that?"

"I hate it," she confessed. "I was still jogging five miles a day when I was eight months pregnant with you. This one though…" She rubbed her belly thoughtfully. "This one is taking everything I've got, plus some."

"Is the baby healthy?" I asked, a question I often asked my dad, but wanted to hear it from her as well.

"Yes. The doctors are happy with the baby's progress, it's my body that's struggling."

I blinked quickly as hot tears filled my eyes. "I'm so sorry, Mom."

"No," she said clearly, sighing again. "I'm sorry, sweetheart. I've been so… stupid. I shouldn't have reacted the way I did when you told me you were pregnant. I was just so angry for you. That you were going to miss out on so much, making the same mistake I did."

"But I'm not, Mom." I gestured to my new home. "Look around. This is my new life. A man who loves me, a new house, and baby girl who will hopefully be born in a month or so. I know this isn't what we planned for, but it's what I want."

My mother stared at me, then nodded slowly. "It's not what we talked about nor planned for you. But I can see how happy you are, sweetheart. And I'm sorry I couldn't be here to help you."

I swallowed hard against the wave of emotion that rose in my throat, clogging my nose and making it difficult to talk.

"I didn't need your help, Mom. I just wanted you to be happy for me. Especially with my baby girl. I'm—" I had to stop and swallow again, the tears getting the better of me now. "I'm so happy I'm pregnant. I really am."

She smiled, and this time I could make out some of the warmth in her eyes that I'd been hoping to see. "I know, sweetheart. Having a daughter, especially when you have one like I did, is a wonderful thing."

"Thanks, Mom." I reached for a tissue and wiped my eyes, "Do you know what you're having?"

She shook her head. "No. We decided not to find out."

I didn't bother bringing up what she'd said at dinner. All of it was in the past.

"So, are we okay? I mean, can we go back to being in each other's lives? I want you to come here, and I want to be able to see you. Go out shopping for baby stuff. All of it."

She grinned this time. "Yes. I'd like that."

"Great!" I said, clapping my hands. "Are you hungry? I can make us something to eat." I groaned as I hauled myself to my feet.

"I'm not really hungry."

I laughed. "Me neither. But my specialist is worried about my weight, so I've gotta eat a bit more."

I walked into the kitchen and pulled out some chocolate that I was sure would tempt her.

I took them back and offered her the box. "I know you like these."

"Thank you." Mom took one, and I grabbed one too, then sat back down on the couch.

"You do look a bit thin," she said.

I laughed. "Yeah. Thin. I'm huge."

Mom shook her head. "No. Your cheeks are sunken, and your arms are too thin."

I sighed. "I didn't mean to lose weight. It's just been difficult to eat, and with all the stress…."

"Make sure you look after yourself," she said. "I'm sure the doctor is right."

I popped the chocolate into my mouth and chewed. "Have you got a good doctor too? Axel said that Dad's insurance should have kicked in for you."

She nodded, the light in her eyes dimming. "Yes, it did. I didn't really want to change doctors, I like mine. But when the pregnancy became high risk, Patrick thought it was better…"

She trailed off and I felt the bone of contention grow.

"So, you're still not happy about Dad and Axel working together?" I asked. May as well talk about everything that was upsetting her. No point leaving it for another day. I wanted everything sorted as quickly as possible.

"It's not that I'm not happy."

"Then what is it?" I asked, forcing myself to reach for the chocolate box I'd set on the coffee table and grab another one for myself. "It's obvious you're not happy about your private health insurance, and that is certainly something I do not understand."

"It's not that I'm not grateful."

I laughed at the expression on her face. "You don't look grateful, Mom. You look like that chocolate in your mouth just turned to ash and you're too polite to spit it out."

Her face twisted up into a bit of a half-smile, half sneer. "I can't help it."

"You can't help what?"

"That I don't like the way we're so entwined in each other's business all of a sudden. Patrick's boss is his best friend but could also be his son-in-law. It's too messy. If something goes wrong between you two or those two, it's going to royally screw up everything. In our lives, Axel's business, Patrick's confidence… everything."

I leaned back against the couch cushion and rubbed my belly, loving the feel of my daughter kicking softly against my left hand. "And if nothing goes wrong, then Dad and Axel are both happy."

My mom frowned at me. "Axel's been too generous. I don't know what to say about all the money he's been throwing at Patrick."

I laughed at that one. "I'm sure you had a lot to say about it at the time, Mom."

"He shouldn't get preferential treatment because they're friends. That's just a recipe for disaster."

I grinned, feeling totally at ease now. My mother had been worried about nothing. She'd probably been sitting at home alone all day, twisting herself in knots.

"Mom, Axel told me that he offered Dad the exact amount he would pay any executive manager. The car, the insurance, it's all standard compensation. If it's a lot more than Dad used to make, then he was wasted in his former role."

Mom was silent for a minute, then nodded. "I told him the same thing about his old job. He worked far too hard for too little."

I grabbed my phone and glanced up at her. "The guys won't be home for hours still. How about we order some take-out and watch a movie?"

Her eyes glistened with unshed tears, then she nodded. "Sounds like fun. What do you want to watch?"

I waggled my eyebrows at her. "What about Father of the Bride, Part 2?"

She laughed at me thinking I was joking, but I wasn't. So, we spent the rest of the afternoon eating popcorn, watching movies, and catching up on the months we'd been apart.

And when Axel called to say he was going to be late, I didn't even mind, because Mom stayed with me. And that's when I knew she'd missed me too.

Chapter 10

Axel

At six pm I texted Chastity to tell her I was going to be late and blamed work for needing to stay back. But when I couldn't concentrate for a single minute more, I went to the gym to work out instead.

I was so furious at Pat I couldn't think straight. He'd advised against taking on a new, pet project that I'd spent a month getting access to. He wanted me to throw all my work away and give up on this deal.

No one had ever spoken to me the way he had, rejecting my idea and telling me it wasn't good enough.

My initial reaction was an explosion of words, and I don't even remember what I said, but I think I might have threatened to fire him. Considering he was my best friend and future father-in-law, everything was far more complicated.

Why did he have to challenge me the way he did? Did he want my company? Did he want us to fail? Did he want to just be a giant pain in my ass for no goddamn reason?

I pumped iron until my arms shook and my chest heaved with the strain. Then I drove around the city until my temper calmed and I felt like it was safe to go home.

When I got there, I sat outside my house for far too long in the car. Who was I going to talk to about this? I couldn't go to Chastity or Pat. Maybe Cheryl would listen?

I dropped my head back against the headrest. Fucking hell. I'd dropped to a new low. I was the boss. I wasn't supposed to be looking for people to whine to. I needed to suck it up and deal with this myself.

Growling with annoyance, I got out of the car and walked towards our new home, my temper dropping as I stepped into the light cast through the front door glass panels. The house had come together beautifully, and Chastity was happy and well. I should be counting my blessings.

But what would happen to us if Patrick and I couldn't sort out our differences? Had hiring him as my second in charge been the right thing to do?

I stood on my doorstep and took a deep breath. I wanted to talk to Chastity about my problem, but how?

The door opened suddenly, and Chastity's beaming face welcomed me home. "You're back." Her gaze swept my clothes. "Did you go to the gym?"

I shrugged, feeling guilty about lying to her, so I told the truth. "Yeah, I had a bad day, so instead of bringing that shit mood home, I tried to work it out myself."

She opened the door wider, her smile not faltering. "Thank you for that. It gave me more time with my mother."

I walked into the hall and put my briefcase down, then realized what she'd said. "Your mother? Did you see her today?" They hadn't been seeing eye-to-eye for months now.

"She's still here. Come and say hello." Chastity grabbed my hand and pulled me down the hallway. "She loves the baby's room, by the way."

I was tugged into our living room, where a woman I barely recognized was sitting at the kitchen table holding her pregnant belly. She was thin and pale and looked not like her usual self.

I nodded at her. "Katherine, it's nice to see you."

She smiled at me, and there was more warmth in her face than I'd ever seen directed at me. "Are you okay, Axel?"

I frowned at her. "Why wouldn't I be?"

"Patrick called. He's worried about you."

I groaned then went straight to the fridge to pull out a cold beer, all pretense gone. I'd hoped to avoid this exact conversation, but Pat dropped me straight into it. "What did he say?"

"You didn't tell me Dad was worried about Axel," Chastity said to her mother, but Katherine didn't respond.

I chugged back some beer, needing the fortification for this conversation. "I didn't want to bring this home to you," I told Chastity, then shook my head. "Church and state." Difficult when things between us were so intricately connected.

Katherine stood up, pale and wan, her belly bulging almost bigger than Chastity's.

"Go on," I said to her. "Tell me that I made a mistake, Katherine. That I should never have hired my best friend, the man that will be my father-in-law." I took another long chug of beer. "I fucked up."

Katherine shook her head. "No. You didn't. You gave Patrick the job he needed. He's been bored for so many years, and you." She stopped and swallowed. "You gave him the chance to do more. Be more."

I ran a hand through my hair. So now she was on my side? When I didn't necessarily want her to be.

"Katherine, that is generous of you. But it doesn't change the fact that Pat is trying to destroy the biggest deal I've ever made. He's making me second-guess everything I've worked so hard for."

Katherine grinned at me and rubbed her belly. "And?"

"What do you mean, and?" Surely, she could see the problem with that.

"I mean, he's your second in charge. He loves you more than anyone."

I put both hands on the counter and stared down at the white marble. "What are you trying to say, Katherine?"

"I'm saying that Patrick's intentions are only to support you. To be worth the money you pay him. If he's telling you to stop and look again, maybe heed his warning."

I glanced up and glared at her. "Seriously? You think he knows better than me what is good for my company?"

Katherine's gaze was steady as she stared at me, looking remarkably like her daughter in that moment.

"What reason would he have to want you to fail? Your company puts food on the table in our house and feeds his daughter, too." She laughed a little to emphasise the point she thought I was dense.

She turned towards Chastity. "It's time for me to go. Can you call your driver for me, sweetheart?"

I hung my head, defeated but still angry. Maybe Katherine was right, and I needed to speak to my second in charge again. "No. Call Pat to come pick you up. He hasn't seen the house yet."

"You want Dad to come to the house now?" Chastity asked, biting her lip as though worried.

I nodded. "Yes. Tell him to come in if he wants to talk. If he doesn't, he can still pick your mom up."

"Okay. Sure." Katherine turned away to use her cell phone and Chastity crept up next to me.

"Are you okay?" she asked, putting her hand on my arm.

I nodded. "Yeah. I think so. Things at work have just been intense lately."

I'd been going after things too hard again. That was becoming clear by the headache building behind my eyes. Chasing those bigger fish that Cheryl had talked about. But with Chastity at home waiting for me every night, I had to leave earlier than I should. Get more done on weekends, or through the night while Chastity slept.

It wasn't easy to balance everything. The company. A partner. Family.

I shook myself and turned towards my beautiful woman, putting my hands around her belly. "How's our baby today? Has she been giving you grief again?"

Chastity slid her hands over mine, moving them to where the baby was kicking. "She's fine. Just getting too big for me to carry her around like this."

"Not long now," I said, leaning forward to kiss Chastity on the lips.

There was another reason I'd been pushing so hard. I wanted everything tied up and settled before the baby was born. Chastity would need me at home, with her. And I wanted to be that support for her.

But currently, I had no idea how I was going to do it all.

"I need a shower," I said, feeling hot and bothered. I was still covered in dried sweat from the gym.

Katherine walked back over to us, her hand pressed to her back. "Patrick said he'll come over and pick me up. He'll be about twenty minutes."

"Perfect timing for me to have a shower, then." I kissed Chastity once more, taking courage and patience from her lips. "Be back soon."

I walked into our bedroom and shut the door, feeling tired to my very bones.

Maybe it was time for a vacation. Somewhere warm, with no internet access. Did such a place exist?

What did Chastity call a vacation at this point? A babymoon? One last holiday before our lives changed forever.

I pulled off my t-shirt and workout sweats, going straight into the newly renovated bathroom. It was clean and bright, and the shower was big enough for Chastity and me to have sex against multiple walls. It was by far one of my favorite places inside the house. The backyard was next. A pool for leisure and exercise.

I stepped beneath the hot spray and sighed at the sensation, wishing the water would wash away all my worries.

Had it been the wrong choice to pursue this deal? Was Pat right?

It hadn't felt like it today when we'd been discussing it. I'd wanted to throttle him for second guessing me, calling me a fool.

I'd regretted hiring him, and had immediately worried what Chastity would think of me for firing her father. It would have ruined so many relationships. Pat's and mine, and perhaps Chastity's and mine.

I wasn't sure having him work with me was worth the risk or the stress.

I didn't know anymore.

After wallowing in how pathetic I was for a few minutes, I scrubbed myself clean, washed my hair and even shaved. May as well face the future well groomed.

When I stepped into the bedroom with a towel wrapped around my waist, Chastity was there, sitting on the bed with the door shut.

I ran my fingers through my still damp hair. "Why do I feel like I'm about to be told off?"

She shook her head. "Oh no, this isn't that at all. I came in to tell you I support you and love you, no matter what. Okay?"

I pulled the towel off my body, quickly dried my hair, then threw it towards the laundry basket.

When I walked towards the closet, I couldn't help but notice the way Chastity's gaze swept over my body. Even in moments of high stress, I loved the connection we shared.

"What do you mean, sweetheart?" I grabbed for a shirt and a comfortable pair of jeans, then pulled the jeans on.

"I mean… you seem to be more worried about the relationships involved in this than the work. I think you're right. You need to separate the two if you can."

I put my arms through the sleeves, then began to button up the shirt. "I don't know if I can, sweetheart. If I want to fire your father, what's that going to do to our relationship? There's a reason Pat and I never worked together before, and that was because I was concerned I'd lose his friendship. Now, we're so much more intertwined than a simple friendship."

He was our baby's grandfather, among other things.

Chastity stood up and walked towards me. "You need to do whatever you need to do. You've been a success because you've worked your ass off and followed your instincts. If you think Dad's wrong, tell him. If you need to fire him, fire him. I'm sure you wouldn't just throw him out on the street with nothing."

"No, of course, not. I could get him a job with some contacts tomorrow."

She smiled at me and lifted her hands to cup my jaw. "Then what are you worried about?"

"I..." What was I worried about the most? "Us. I don't want anything I say or do with my company to affect you and me."

She kissed me and said, "It won't. I'll make sure of it. I'm proud of you. So do what you've gotta do."

The doorbell rang and I turned towards it. "Your dad's here."

She nodded and took my hand in hers. "Let's go, then."

Chapter 11

Axel

Chastity walked ahead to the front door and opened it for her father. He spoke to her quietly, and my gut churned. What the hell was I going to do about this?

Part of me wanted to leave. To avoid the whole situation. But the bigger part of me told me to man up and face whatever needed to be done.

"Come see the baby's room. It's my favorite place to be in the house. Although, the kitchen is pretty amazing, too." Chastity was waxing lyrical about her happiness with the house.

She was telling her dad about the new floors, the plans for the backyard, and I still hadn't stepped out of my bedroom.

I took a breath and was just about to step out when Katherine pushed open the door to pop her head in.

"Are you still in here?"

I nodded. "Yeah, why?"

She smiled at me, and there was a hesitancy in the smile I didn't usually see from her. "You're really worried about this, aren't you?"

I glanced away, still not sure about this woman. "Yeah, I am."

"Why?"

"Why?" I repeated, feeling exasperated. "Because everything I care about is on the line. Chastity, Pat, my company."

She smiled serenely this time, rubbing her belly in rhythmic circular motions. "I like your list of priorities. That's how it should be."

I frowned at her. "What do you mean?"

"You said, 'Chastity, Patrick then your company.' It may have been accidental, but that's how you see it in order of importance. And that's how it should be. Your wife, or partner. You best friend. Your job."

I sighed and scrubbed my hands over my face. "Katherine, I—"

"No, wait. Axel. I'm trying to pay you a compliment, not upset you. I…" She stopped, then frowned. "It's no secret I haven't always liked you."

I huffed out a laugh at that one. "Really? No way."

"You're the sort of man who tends to chew on girls and spit them out, and I was scared for Chastity in the beginning."

I opened my mouth to rebut her, but she spoke over top of me. "But I was wrong."

My jaw dropped.

She grinned at me. "There. I said it. I was wrong. About you. About you and Chastity. My daughter is the happiest I've ever seen her, and you're obviously a good man. A good provider. A great friend, or Patrick wouldn't have kept you around for a decade."

I sighed. "Why do I feel like there's a but coming?"

"No but," she said, shaking her head. "I just ask that you listen to Patrick the same way you have on all the other issues you two have faced. He loves you. My daughter loves you. And my granddaughter is going to love you too."

Katherine stopped talking and I could see the tears shimmering in her eyes.

A strange tightness wove around my chest, and I nodded at the woman who I'd been at odds with since the moment I met her. "Thank you, Katherine."

She nodded and she may have wanted to say something else, but that's when Chastity and Pat found us.

"What are you two doing in the bedroom?" Pat asked, his face lighting up with humor. "If I didn't know you both so well, I might be jealous."

"You?" Chastity huffed at him, nudging her mom out of the way softly to come stand next to me. "I'd just start to worry that Axel really does have a thing for pregnant women, and it's not just me."

I wrapped my arms around her and kissed her hair. "It's just you, sweetheart."

She cuddled in, then silence fell over us. When I looked up, Pat was sharing a strange look with Katherine.

"Should we take this party back to the living room?" he suggested.

"Sure," I agreed. "Want a beer?"

"Yeah, that would be great," Pat said, and we all walked back into the living room.

I got us beers and the women sat on the couches, both holding their large bellies.

I handed Pat the bottle and he said, "How about you show me the backyard? Chastity said you want to put in a pool."

"Yeah. That's a good idea." Get away from the girls and have a proper talk.

I opened the French doors, let Patrick through, then shut them behind him. "There's chairs beneath the tree," I told him. "If you want somewhere quiet."

It would be dark too, which would help both of us be able to speak freely.

We wandered off the back porch and took a seat on either side of the massive tree in the backyard. The sun had gone down, and the shroud of darkness fell around us.

"It's a beautiful house, Axel. Chastity is very lucky."

I glanced over at my best friend. "I'm the lucky one, Pat. She's amazing."

Silence fell again.

Should I start, or would he?

When he didn't speak, I decided to forge ahead. After all, I was his boss. "Pat, I'm sorry about what happened today. I behaved badly."

And I had. I'd never yelled at an employee like that.

Pat sighed as he drank his beer. "You might be right. Working together and being family might be too much."

I settled further in the chair, relaxing against the back. "How do people do it? Keep everything separate."

"I don't think that's so much the key," Patrick said quietly. "Some of the best teams in the world are related. Father and son. Brothers. They make it work because they're related, not in spite of it."

It sounded like he'd thought about this. "What do you mean?"

"Well, our friendship makes me more honest with you, more likely to tell you the truth."

That didn't really help. "Pat—"

"No. Think about it. You can hire any guy to be your second. Pay him a fortune to bow and scrape and work his ass off. But he doesn't care if you lose twenty million dollars. He doesn't care if your company goes ass up. He'll just move on to the next job. But you're my family, Axel. Your success feeds my daughter. Will pay for my granddaughter's education. And I'll be damned if I stand by and let you make a mistake that could ruin you. I won't do it. You can fire me for being a stubborn asshole who won't let you make a deal I think is shit. I won't lie to you. I won't feed your ego. I won't do it, Axel."

I swallowed hard and set the beer bottle on the grass next to the chair.

I opened my mouth to speak then swallowed and shut my mouth again. Was he right? Would Taylor have stuck her neck out when I'd yelled that I wanted the deal?

Probably not.

Pat had.

I groaned. "Do you really think it's that bad a deal?"

"Hell, yes. I ran the numbers. Let me show you tomorrow. If I'm wrong, you can fire me."

I turned towards him. "I don't want to fire you, but I'm not sure I can stop myself from yelling at you if you go up against me like that again."

I'd been so angry, treated my friend like shit, and I hated myself for what I'd said.

Pat chuckled. "Yeah? And?"

"I don't want it to be like that between us. Yelling and screaming. Feeling..."

"What? Angry?"

"Yes!" I hated feeling so out of control.

He laughed. "Bud, you're my best friend. I don't care if you yell and scream and throw a chair at me. I'm gonna tell you straight up what I think. It's up to you if you want someone kissing your ass or covering it. Because I'm only here to do one of those things."

I stood up and reached my hand out to my friend. "So, you'll keep working for me?"

Pat put his hand in mine to shake, and I pulled him up to his feet. "Yes. But only if you can handle me giving you the truth, because I'm not gonna lie to you, Axel. Not for any money."

Pulling him in close, I hugged him hard. "You're a good friend, Pat."

"And you're a great boss, Axel. But you need to learn to take advice."

We turned and walked back towards the house. "Yeah, I do. And I could probably use a little more."

I stepped up on the porch and glanced inside. Chastity was laughing, chatting with her mom. The light made her hair glow gold, her skin luminescent.

"Tell me what you need," Pat said, standing next to me on the porch.

Shoulder to shoulder. My brother in arms.

"I need to... slow down. But I don't know how. I hired the terrifying trio to take my workload down a notch, then got you to take the rest of the stress. But Cheryl started funneling these new projects to me and I saw the potential for growth and..."

"You can't stop. You're a workaholic. I've always said it."

I punched my friend in the shoulder. "Shut up. I need help, not your shit."

Pat chuckled loudly. "Look, you need a vacation, friend. It's obvious. You're about to have a baby and you're killing yourself for what… another million? Take Chastity away to Hawaii or something. Get some rest. I promise your empire will still be here when you get back."

I scrubbed my hands over my face. "Fuck, Pat. How have you done this for so many years? Managed a kid, work?"

And he'd done more than that. Stayed healthy, fit. Dated women. Climbed the corporate ladder.

He laughed. "I didn't manage an entire company the way you do, but yeah, it's fucking hard, man." He reached for the handle and opened the door. "Now, you tell Chastity you're gonna take her for a vacation and I'll convince Cheryl to back off for a few years until my granddaughter is old enough."

He opened the door, but that's when we heard a pained moan and a shout. "Dad! Quick!"

We bolted inside and Chastity was standing over her mother, where Katherine was leaning over on her side, clutching her belly.

"Something's wrong!" Katherine cried. "The baby."

"I'm calling an ambulance," I said to the room, while Pat knelt down next to his woman.

I put the cell phone to my ear and dialed nine-one-one, Katherine's moans turning to screams in my ears.

They came within five minutes, buckling Katherine on a gurney and Pat in the ambulance with her.

Chastity began to cry as soon as they left and I held her tightly, thanking God for our blessings and the healthy baby still in Chastity's belly.

"What if the baby dies?" Chastity whispered to me an hour later. Katherine had wanted Chastity to stay home and rest and the uncertainty was getting to her.

Patrick had promised to call as soon as he had news, but if Katherine was taken into surgery, I knew Chastity would want to go to the hospital. So, we waited on the couch, having not moved from where we'd collapsed after they left.

"Don't talk like that," I told her. "They'll call soon."

When my cell phone rang, we both jumped. It was Patrick. I reached for it and answered.

"Pat! Is everything okay?"

Chapter 12

Chastity

My heart was thundering in my chest as I stared at the cell phone. It was Dad. "Oh, please have news on Mom."

Axel continued talking to my dad. "Hey, let me put you on speaker." Then he pressed the button and held the cell phone out in front of him so I could hear. "Is everything okay?"

"How's Mom? How's the baby?" I called out, digging my nails into Axel's arm where I sat on the couch, pressed into his side.

"They're fine. They're both fine," Dad said.

I exhaled, relief flowing over me in a massive wave. "Oh, thank God." I reached for the phone and took it out of Axel's hand. "What happened, Dad?"

"False labor, they think. The baby isn't doing so well, and Kaiti has pre-eclampsia, which we already knew was going to be a risk. But as Kaiti's only thirty weeks, so they're going to try and keep the baby in there as long as possible."

My hand flew up to her mouth. "What does that mean? Is she home?"

Hopefully she was already in bed with a book or curled up, watching a movie.

"No. They're going to keep her in here, on bed rest. Keep her hydrated, monitor the baby and Kaiti's blood pressure. If anything happens and she gets worse… well…"

"Well, what?" I demanded, standing up so I could move around. "What are they going to do?" I'd read a little on pre-eclampsia and it was terrible for the baby and the mother.

"They said they'll do an emergency c-section and get the baby out," my father said, all in a rush. He sounded stressed, and by the sounds of it, he should be.

My eyes filled with tears. "But she's only thirty weeks." The baby was only one and a half, maybe two pounds in weight. He or she would have a tough road ahead if the delivery was this early.

"Yeah, but your mom's strong. And thanks to the healthcare Axel gave us when I took the job, the hospital said they can keep her in and look after her until she delivers. Whether that's tomorrow, or in two months."

I looked towards my beautiful man and gave him a grateful smile. "Then I suppose Axel's job did come in handy, Dad."

I leaned down and kissed him where he still sat on the couch. He'd made sure my parents were taken care of, even if they hadn't always seen eye to eye.

Axel shrugged, always the modest one.

Dad chuckled softly. "It's come in more than handy, sweetheart. We bought a new house a month back, thanks to this job. I can finally give your mom the family home she's always wanted. So, yeah, I owe Axel more than he knows. Which, by the way, friend, if you're still listening, is more proof why I'd never lie to you or mislead you. I would never have been able to afford the house we wanted on my old salary, and my old health insurance would never have covered Kaiti's condition. So, thank you."

Axel stared at me, obviously overwhelmed at the compliment.

I shoved the phone at him and whispered, "Say something."

Axel coughed to clear his throat. "Yeah. Of course. No problem, Pat. Let's talk about it when you come back to work. Take a few days off if you need to."

"No need," Dad said. "I have to go home and pack a bag for Kaiti, then I'm on my own until they call me. I'll go crazy waiting at home, and Kaiti doesn't want me in the hospital twenty-four-seven anyway, so I'll see you tomorrow."

Axel coughed again. "Send Katherine our best wishes, Pat. I hope everything's okay."

"Yeah, me too. Better go. Gotta get Kaiti her hospital bag. Lucky she'd already packed it. See you tomorrow."

Dad hung up and I collapsed back on the couch next to Axel.

He ran his hand over our baby bump, and I cupped our baby too. "We're so lucky, Axel. I know I've complained about being sick and exhausted, and the size of a whale, but Mom is really unwell. And the baby could die. Pre-eclampsia is really serious if it isn't managed properly."

"But it is being managed," Axel said, though he continued to press his hands into my belly. "Though you're right, we are lucky, sweetheart. Lucky to have each other, and lucky for this little miracle."

He bent his head and kissed my bump, then stood up. "God, what a day. I think I'm ready for an early night."

I glanced across the room at the wall clock. "It's only ten o'clock."

He twisted around to stare at me. "Do you wanna stay up?"

"No," I sighed, pushing myself to my feet. I napped every day just so I could stay up long enough to see him after work. "No, I'd love an early night. But I know you've been getting up to work through the nights and early mornings too. Just checking you're okay to go to bed now."

Axel stared at me like he was shocked with what I'd said.

"What?" I asked.

"I didn't realize you knew."

"Knew what? That you left bed in the middle of the night to go work. Of course, I did." I barely slept an hour before needing to wake up, readjust the pillows or roll over. I knew he left, and I knew he was working. I could hear the clickity click of his typing in the quiet of the night.

"Why didn't you say something?"

I shrugged. "It wasn't a big deal." I took his hand and tugged him towards the bedroom. "Let's go get ready for bed."

I walked into our huge master bedroom and began to undress, sighing when I unhooked my bra and let my heavy breasts fall against my belly. "My boobs are so big now."

Axel chuckled from his side of the room. "One of the many things I love about your pregnant body."

"Oh?" I glared at him. "What else do you like about it? The swollen ankles? The huge belly? The acne?"

My pimples had gone nuts, and I couldn't even bend over to tie my shoelaces. All my flexibility in sex was gone, which I hated.

I pulled back the covers and climbed into bed naked and hot.

Axel slid in too, pulling me into his arms. "I love your huge belly," he whispered into my ear, running his hand over the flesh. "And I'd take you right this minute, if you'd let me, so none of my attraction for you has disappeared." He thrust against me to make his point, his cock hard against my ass.

I closed my eyes. "I love you."

He laughed and kissed my hair, knowing that I'd gone past my sex window. My body turns off around nine pm, unfortunately. "I love you, too."

We lay in the silence for a minute, and just as I was beginning to fall into the darkness of sleep, Axel said, "Hey, how come you haven't said anything about my working so much? I thought you'd be annoyed or something."

I pulled myself up from the depths of sleep. I had to focus because Axel's tone told me he needed to talk, but I couldn't open my eyes.

"I'm not annoyed. How can I be?" I asked him with a soft laugh. "You bought this incredible house for us, and you provide for a hundred families as well." Like my parents.

When I realized that Axel had been deliberately hiding the amount of work he did, I'd felt terrible. He shouldn't have to pretend he had balance in his life when he didn't. He had to work a stupid amount of hours to be the success he was, and I was proud of him.

When he didn't say anything, I continued, "I'm sorry I made you feel like you had to hide your work." I ran my hand over his fingers where he gripped my hip. "I'm so proud of you and your success. And I'm sorry I was such a bitch about it all those months ago. I was selfish to think that I could have all your time when so many people count on you."

And work made Axel happy, that was obvious. If I tried to take that away from him, what sort of partner would that make me?

"Thank you for saying that," Axel whispered, and this time I heard the sadness in his voice.

I groaned with the strain but managed to roll onto my back, then roll again to face him. "What's wrong? You sound sad."

Which wasn't like Axel, not at all.

"I'm not sad, it's just…" He stopped and sighed.

"What's going on, hon?" I asked, leaning forward to kiss his lips. "You can tell me anything."

And I would try not to argue or get mad, even if he suddenly wanted to go back to working all weekend, every weekend again. I wouldn't like it, but I wouldn't complain.

"It's just that, I suppose I'm feeling a bit lost at work. Since hiring all the support staff, I don't feel like I have enough to do."

"What do you mean?" I asked, confused. "What are you doing at three am on the computer if you're not working?" Because this, I had to know!

"I'm working. I didn't mean that. I've found new things to do, but I'm not enjoying it as much as I used to. I don't think I've figured out where I want to be yet."

I absorbed what he said and took a minute to put it all together. "Is that why you and Dad got into a fight at work?"

"Sort of. I wanted to move ahead with a deal that I'd put together for months, and he thinks it's a bad idea. So, I suppose it's a symptom of me feeling completely lost."

"Let me see if I've got it," I said slowly. "You've set up this awesome company and have delegated your responsibilities to people that seem to be doing okay at them, but now you're not sure what to do?"

He sighed. "Kind of. Yeah. Maybe it's time for a vacation."

I grinned into the darkness. "A babymoon?"

"You know we haven't even gone on a honeymoon yet," he reminded me.

I laughed. "Yeah, we do everything backwards. So, you think you could take a couple of days off to relax and maybe decide what you want to do next?"

I was dying to get away and spend some quality time with Axel. It had been months since we'd had more than a few minutes here and there, snatches of time around the renovating, studying and work.

"I'd need to speak to Pat, make sure he's okay with us going, considering your mom's status."

"Oh, yeah, you're right," I said, biting my lip. "I don't want to miss the baby being born."

"We could stay local, or at least within a few hours' travel time. Cancun, maybe?" Axel suggested. "Then, if they need us, we could fly straight back."

I gasped. "Really? You think I'm bikini-ready?"

He reached over and cupped my face. "Absolutely. So, you want to go away? I'll organize it tomorrow and we can leave as soon as possible."

I tried not to squeal with excitement as I nodded. "Oh, yes, please. I love our new home, but I miss spending time with you, so if we could go away and relax just for a bit before the baby comes, I'd love it so much."

"It's a good idea," he whispered. "Time for me to reassess a few things, and time to enjoy just us before we become a family."

"Perfect," I said, feeling the tears fill my eyes again. How had I gotten so lucky?

Then he kissed me and in that one moment, it felt like everything was going to be okay.

Chapter 13

Chastity

WITHIN THIRTY-SIX HOURS, WE WERE PACKED AND ON A PRIVATE PLANE, flying down to Cancun for our babymoon.

"I can't believe this!" I cried happily, staring out the window. "We're really going on a vacation." Together. Just us. The last opportunity before the baby came.

There had been a few boxes to tick before we left, and we'd gotten everything organized in record time. Mom was stable and her doctor didn't anticipate having to act for at least a few more weeks, baring complications.

Dad and the management trio eagerly took on the role of looking after the company in Axel's absence—under the watchful eye of Cheryl, of course. And I'd gotten my specialist's okay to fly at almost thirty-five weeks, because we said we'd be back in five days or less.

"Have you spoken to Dad today?" I asked him.

"Yeah, I called before we left. Your mom's medication seems to be working and her blood pressure is down, but they're still keeping her at the hospital."

I grinned at him. "Yeah, she messaged me this morning. I think she's driving everyone nuts, but I'm glad she's there." She would have preferred to be home of course, but she was in the safest place for her and the baby. And she knew it. "Thank you again for making sure she has the best care."

Axel smiled. "My pleasure."

The flight to Cancun was quick and easy, and before long we were sitting on lounges beside the resort pool with drinks. Axel had some sort of whiskey cocktail, and I had a pretty mocktail with a pineapple chunk and an umbrella.

"Ahhh, this is paradise." I sighed, closing my eyes and loving the feel of the sunshine on my belly. Axel had convinced me to wear the bikini I'd brought as a joke. Even though my boobs overflowed the cups, and my belly was huge.

He said he loved it and who was I to argue? After all, nothing said "this guy is taken" more than a heavily pregnant woman glued to his side.

"Would you like anything to eat, ma'am?" a man asked someone close by.

I lifted my hat off my head and glanced up. The guy with the tray was talking to me. "Oh, no, thank you."

He nodded and walked away.

I looked around the resort, noticing the lack of people. "Is this place usually this quiet?"

"Well, it is September, which is low season," Axel said. "But this resort does have lower numbers due to their large suites."

"So, you spent more to stay at a place that has limited rooms and limited guests." I think I was starting to work it out.

"Yeah, that's about right," he said with a shrug, his naked shoulders moving in a sexy way that had my lower body warming up for later.

I grinned at him. "Cool." I lay back, put my hat over my face and soaked in the atmosphere.

At dinner we had fresh seafood and more drinks, chatting like we used to. "I've missed you," I told him.

When his face fell like he was upset, I reached over the table and grabbed his hand. "I didn't mean it in a bad way. It's just, you know… we spent so much time together over Christmas break, then with my studying, and your job, time was harder to get. Then the renovations and everything. It's amazing, though, and I love our life. But I miss just sitting with you and talking, that's all. It wasn't meant to be a negative."

He twirled his fingers around so I could hold his hand properly. "I know what you mean. It was easy in the beginning. Just enjoying each other's company, thinking we only had a week or two together."

"I'm much happier now, knowing we have forever," I told him, grinning happily. "But I just wanted to say thank you for this. I know work has your head in a bit of a spin, but you're still taking this time to spend with me."

The baby kicked, and I ran a hand over her little feet. "Ouch! She's getting so strong."

He smiled at me, but I could feel the tension in him now. "Hey, I'm sorry if I upset you. I didn't mean to."

Quite the opposite, actually.

"No, you didn't. It's okay. I'm just in a bit of a strange place at the moment. Sorry."

I squeezed his hand. "How about we go back to the room after dinner? I want to show you something."

"Oh, yeah?" He asked, taking a sip of his beer.

I nodded and crunched on the salad in front of me. I'd been aching for intimacy with Axel for a few days. Like we used to, where I adored his body and made him scream.

I wasn't sure he'd want that from me with this big belly distracting his thoughts and attention, but I was going to try.

"Well, I'm pretty much done," Axel said, his eyes now burning with the desire I'd been hoping to see. "You ready to show me?"

I nodded. "Yep. Let's go." I pushed my plate away and stood up, grabbing my man's hand.

We hurried through the restaurant, finding the elevator and step-ping inside. "Are you going to give me a clue?" Axel whispered into my ear as he pushed the button to our floor. "Is it a new watch or something I can wear?"

I laughed at him. "Just because you gave me a credit card to pay the food bills with, doesn't mean I'm going to spend it on anything else."

He drew back and blinked at me. "What do you mean?"

I swallowed hard. "I mean… I'm sorry. No, I haven't bought you anything."

"Because you don't have access to money yet. Shit. I am so sorry." He stepped back and ran a frazzled hand through his hair. "I thought you understood that card was for anything you want to buy. Stuff for the baby. Clothes. A gym membership. Anything."

I frowned at him. "Thanks, but I'm not really comfortable spending your money like that."

The doors dinged open and the reasons for coming upstairs were fading fast.

Axel took my hand and tugged me out of the elevator and to the large, red door that was the entrance to our suite. "Sweetheart, you can't work now, and probably won't want to work until the baby is much older. I hope, anyway. My money is officially your money now."

He opened the door and I walked into the suite. This conversation was officially one I didn't want to have. I wanted to be on my knees, sucking his cock, and enjoying the pure joy of his body, not talking about money.

The door shut behind me and I took action. I untied the halter-neck dress from behind my neck and let it shimmy down my body until it hit the floor.

Then I spun around, ready to get on my knees for him and prove how much I loved him.

But he was already on his knees, staring at me.

He wasn't undressed, he still wore his shirt and slacks and was down on the ground.

"Um, what are you…"

He pulled a small black box out of his slacks and held it in his hand. "Chastity, I love you more than anything in this world."

He stopped, and I swallowed hard, wanting to cover up my naked-ness, but feeling like that would destroy the atmosphere he was trying to create.

"I love you too," I whispered, stepping closer.

Was he really doing what I thought he was doing?"

"No one has ever loved me or challenged me or made me smile the way you do. You're the most beautiful person, inside and out."

He opened the ring box and I gasped, covering my mouth with my hand. "Oh my God."

Inside the box was the most glorious engagement ring. It had a huge, round white diamond at its center, surrounded by tiny pink diamonds.

"Chastity, would you marry me? Be my wife, as you're already the mother of our child?"

Tears welled up in my eyes as my heart soared.

It was too soon, wasn't it?

Our daughter kicked inside my belly, reminding me that it wasn't too soon. We were a family, and Axel wanted us to be husband and wife. What would be more perfect than that?

"Yes," I whispered, nodding my head in case he didn't hear me. "Yes. Of course, I'll marry you."

He jumped to his feet and rushed me, kissing me hard as I sobbed with joy.

"Thank you" he whispered, pulling back to take the ring from its box and grabbing my left hand. "I went a little bigger on the sizing just in case, but we can get it resized anytime you like."

He slid the ring onto my finger, where it lay snug against my knuckle. "It's perfect."

"No. You're perfect," he said, reaching over to cup my face and kiss me. "Now, our house will be our home. My money will be our money. And our daughter will have my name. I hope?"

I grinned at him. "Only if I get it too."

He chuckled. "Of course."

"Oh, Axel." I threw my arms around him. "A baby, a house, and a proposal in less than a year. Are we crazy?"

He hugged me tight. "Yep. Totally crazy. Now... what were you going to show me?"

He drew back and raised an eyebrow at me in question.

"Oh!" I dropped to my knees and unbuttoned and unzipped his trousers. I wanted him now more than ever.

"What are you—?"

I looked up at him and grinned as I took his cock out. "Showing you how much I love you."

I put my left hand around his girth, admiring the way my new ring twinkled in the lights, then I sucked the head into my mouth.

He groaned, sliding his hand into my hair. "You don't need to do that. Are you comfortable down there?"

I came off and looked up at him. "Very comfortable, actually. But I can stop if you like?"

He shook his head from side to side. "No. Please…" He tugged on my hair, and I grinned as I moved forward once more.

I was very comfortable on my knees actually, and as I took him back into my mouth and listened to the sound of his moans, I got squirmy and wet between my legs.

I dropped one hand between my thighs, running my fingers over my panties and enjoying the sensations of pleasure pulsing up from my clit.

Axel groaned and tugged my hair back. "Bed?"

I shook my head. "No. Here."

I sat on the floor, pushed my panties down my legs, then rolled over and stuck my ass in the air.

It was dirty and fast, but Axel didn't disappoint me. He knelt down behind me and slid his cock between my thighs, sliding it over my throbbing flesh, checking for my readiness.

I ached for him so badly.

"Come on! Please!" I urged, wiggling back against him

He pressed the head to my slit and thrust in. I gasped at the pleasure and the pressure as he forged inside of me.

I rocked on his cock, loving the feeling of him against me.

"You okay?" he called out.

I nodded and moaned. "Yes. Don't stop."

And he took me right there there—hard and fast—on the carpet. Writhing, aching, needing him so badly, until we were both screaming out our orgasms.

Best proposal night ever.

Chapter 14

Axel

After I proposed and fucked Chastity on the ground like some sort of animal, we lay on the carpet, trying to catch our breath.

Fuck, that was hot but so unexpected.

And probably incredibly uncomfortable for my very pregnant fiancé.

I pulled her into my arms. "Are you okay? Did I hurt you?"

She turned to look up at me, her face pink, sweaty and radiant. "Not at all. That was amazing." She groaned as she rolled onto her hands and knees again. "But I think I need to get up. Can we move this celebration to the bed?"

I jumped to my feet and put out my hand to help her to her feet.

"Oh, I'm okay. It's easier if I do it," Chastity said, getting slowly up. "Phew."

I gestured to the carpet. "Are you sure that was okay?" I was feeling guilty as hell, even though I was pretty sure she'd instigated it all. The details were a little fuzzy now.

She laughed. "Are you kidding me? I was the one on my knees and too impatient to get to the bed. So, thank you for ignoring the whole pregnant belly thing and just, you know…"

She faded off and it was my turn to laugh. "What? Just fucking you?" I grabbed her and kissed her. "My pleasure."

She giggled as she walked towards the bedroom. "Just gonna pee, then I'll get into bed."

"Okay, sweetheart." I was so tempted to use the energy buzz currently pushing through my bloodstream for something else. A gym session. Work, maybe.

But this was a vacation, and I was trying to learn how to just relax.

I heard the toilet flush, so I grabbed some bottles of water and headed towards the bed.

"You wanna put a movie on?" I asked, grabbing the remote and pointing it towards the huge smart TV opposite the bed.

"Sure," she said, flopping onto the California king mattress. "But don't expect me to stay awake for it. That orgasm was awesome. So strong, I can barely keep my eyes open."

She crawled up the bed and put her head on the fluffy white pillows.

She looked like a goddess amongst the blankets. A rounded, heavily pregnant goddess.

"Damn, you're beautiful," I said, sitting on the mattress and running my hand over her ass and up the curve of her spine.

"Hmmmm, I love you. Can we call everyone in the morning and tell them?"

Tell everyone? Oh, right. "You mean about us being engaged? Absolutely."

I crawled over and lay down facing her, then swept her long hair off her face. "We could steal off to Vegas and get married this week, if you want."

Her eyes opened slowly, though they were unfocused. "You want to be married to me that badly?"

"Yes. The sooner the better."

I'd wanted to propose for months. But I wanted her to be happy, and in a good place mentally before I popped the question.

Her eyes closed as she sighed. "I love that. Thank you. But I'd really want my parents there."

I kissed her cheek. "You sleep."

"Are you going to work?" she whispered.

"No, I'll just lay here," I said. "I'm jumping out of my skin, excited, though."

She was going to be my wife. I'd never felt better.

"Okay. But I don't mind. You do what you've gotta do. I need to sleep though, I'm sorry."

I glanced down at her and kissed her again. "You sleep."

And she did, snoring softly within moments. I grinned to myself. There was nothing like a strong orgasm to knock you out and guarantee a good night's sleep.

Usually I'd be right alongside her, ready to pass out from the bliss. But tonight, I was jumping.

I got up and got dressed, buzzing to do something with the energy. Maybe a run? Yeah. Why not? I hadn't gone for a run in weeks, choosing instead to train for twenty minutes, and get back into work.

But I'd done too much of that lately. I was making mistakes. Like that deal Pat had saved me from closing on. He'd been right. I'd gone into work yesterday and he spelled it out.

The business I'd wanted to buy was drowning in so much debt, it was possible I wouldn't have been able to dig myself out for a very long time. Pat may have saved my whole company.

And although I was more grateful than I could say, I owed Pat that house he wanted for his family. It was the wake-up call I'd needed.

I had the people to delegate to, and while I found my footing in my new CEO role, I had to take a step back and reassess.

Why did I keep pushing so hard? I'd reached the goals I set for myself years ago, but as with all goal setting, once the bar was reached, there was always something else to shoot for.

A higher profit. More staff. Bigger fish.

But was that something I still wanted now that I had Chastity.

I was going to be married, with a baby daughter. I wanted to stay fit and healthy for them. I wanted to provide for them, but that didn't mean being absent at home.

Chastity was saying now that she accepted that I needed to work my ass off to keep my company, but did I really? Did I have to kill myself to keep the status quo? To pay off my house. To put food on the table.

No.

I had enough money to never work again. To have five children, provide them an Ivy League education and buy them all houses. So, did I really need to die on the sword of the corporate world?

I pulled on some joggers, a clean t-shirt and some running shoes, then I headed out.

I got a lot of weird, confused looks from staff and other guests, probably assuming I didn't belong there. But I just popped my air pods into my ears, cranked up the music, and took off.

It was just at sunset and the sun was melding into the water in a mess of orange and yellows.

I jogged over the brush and onto the beach, hitting my stride and taking off down the beach while some techno instrumental played in my ears.

Why did I work the way I did? I'd always put it down to a simple drive to succeed. Money.

But was it really that?

Could I walk away tomorrow? Sell the company, pay any debt, and invest what was left? I certainly had the assets to do it. But would that make me happy? Would Chastity be content with me just being around the house all day. What would I even do?

I reached a natural end of the beach, stopped and turned to look back the way I had come. I had no idea how far I'd run, but my brow was slick with sweat, my breathing was labored, and my heart banged like a bongo drum in my chest.

"Time to go back."

My legs didn't want to move, but I pushed them to start going again, and once I found my rhythm on the wet sand, it was easy to follow my footprints back to the hotel.

I'd run further than I realized, so I took a moment and sat on the beach, staring up at the moon.

I checked my phone that was in my pocket. Chastity hadn't messaged or called. Good. She was hopefully still fast asleep.

I put my hands behind me, digging them into the sand and took a few deep breaths.

Could I get rid of all responsibilities and live day to day without work? Would I find a hobby? Or a renovation project, maybe? Was that something that interested me?

What about mentoring another young businessperson? Or trading on the stock market?

I groaned at the possibilities rolling around in my head.

I loved my job and my company. I didn't want to sell it. Or stop working. Not at the moment, anyway. Maybe once the baby arrived, I'd feel differently, but at the moment it felt like everything was more difficult and wasn't giving me the same satisfaction it did before I hired help.

Maybe I needed to back off on the big acquisitions, and just manage. Work with Pat closer.

I didn't know.

I needed to talk to Chastity. She seemed to have a better insight into business and life than I did sometimes. How, I didn't know. Or maybe it was because she had the advantage of youth?

I got up and brushed the sand off my pants. This had been a good idea to come down to Cancun and rest, relax, reassess.

Chastity was here to enjoy her last few weeks as a woman before she became a mother, which gave me lots of room to spoil her.

I went back to the hotel, up to the suite, and had a long shower in the main bathroom, avoiding the ensuite so I didn't wake her. The place we'd gotten was a three-bedroom suite. None of the one-bedrooms were available, and they tended to be too small anyway.

When I was clean, dry, and finally tired, I crept back into our bedroom.

She was still asleep, and I stood in the doorway, wondering if it was best that I go into the other room. I might disturb her, and that's not what she needed.

I turned towards the other bedrooms and Chastity called out, "Hey. You coming to sleep now?"

I twisted back to her smiling face. "Are you sure you're okay with me sleeping here? I might disturb you."

She flicked back the covers. "Are you kidding? This bed is huge. Jump in."

I walked across the room, my naked feet sinking into the plush carpet.

"Plus, you just proposed, remember?" she said, rolling over to present her ass to me. "I think that requires at least a few cuddles to celebrate."

I chuckled as I slid up behind her. "I think so too." I pressed myself into her warmth.

"I love you," she said, shoving her ass back at me.

"I love you too." I returned, sliding my hand around her waist to cup her belly. "Both of you."

"Mmmm... Night."

She fell asleep again, and I lay there counting my blessings. One. Two.

The two girls in front of me were the two most important things in my life now. I needed to sort out what I wanted to do for work, but it wasn't a pressing issue.

I had plenty of everything, so maybe I could slow down for a little bit. It wouldn't kill me, right?

I closed my eyes and drifted off to sleep, a childhood memory tugging at me just long enough to make me curious, but not concrete enough to sink my teeth into.

I'd work it out in the morning.

Chapter 15

Chastity

Axel spoiled me tremendously over the next few days as we enjoyed our vacation in Cancun. Our resort was near a large, upscale mall, so we went shopping and bought beautiful clothes for the baby and several things for me, even though I thought it was a waste of money to buy maternity clothes now. Axel still wanted me to be comfortable.

And happy.

That's what he said, all the time. "I want you to be happy." It blew my mind that my happiness was his goal, and I was. Deliriously happy. How could I not be? I had a man who loved me and had proposed marriage.

A man I loved who had fathered my daughter, still growing in my womb. Things couldn't be better.

On the last morning before we left to return home, we were sitting at breakfast when Axel brought up a topic that I felt he'd been keeping inside for far too long.

"Can I chat with you about something before we head back?"

"Sounds serious," I said, my stomach swooping in an anxious way. "Is this about us?"

He shook his head. "No, not at all. I want your advice about something."

"Of course," I said, relief sweeping over me as I took a sip of my freshly squeezed pineapple juice. "Tell me what's going on."

He sighed and leaned forward, gripping the small table with both hands. "I... don't know what to do about work. I'm feeling useless there, in my own company. It's strange."

I gaped at him, then put the glass down. "Useless? You?" I fluffed my new pink dress over my baby bump and settled my hands over my daughter. "How is that possible?"

I settled into the chair, trying to find a comfortable position. This was going to be a long conversation, I could already tell.

We had six hours before we had to go to the airport, so we had time to hash this out. And with the waiters hovering around, we also had as much food and drinks available as we wanted to consume.

"Yes, me," he said, dropping his head and running an agitated hand through his hair. "I walk around the office, watching everyone else perform the tasks I used to do. Coupled with the fact that I'm finding I don't have as may responsibilities now, it's weird."

I grinned at him. "You've delegated too well, is that what you're saying?"

"Well, yes. I think so."

I reached for a grape and popped it into my mouth, the sweetness exploding in my mouth the moment I crunched down on it. "You know you had to hire three new graduates and a kick-ass manager to do the work you used to do as one person? That's insane."

He laughed and pushed himself back in the chair. "I know, you've joked about it before. They're killing it, though. Doing all of my jobs and doing them well. I've heard from Cheryl the four of them don't even need to work weekends, which is great for them."

He didn't sound happy about it though. "But what? You're missing it? The hours? The weekends, the nights, the huge amount of work you used to do?"

Axel ran a hand over his face and groaned like he was frustrated.

I opened my legs so I could move forward on my chair, my belly too big now to sit comfortably practically anywhere.

"Look, I get it. It was your life for, what, twenty years? Of course, you miss it. The adrenaline. The success. Ticking off jobs and dealing with international meetings, and travel, and…" I threw my hands around. "All the millions of other things you do that I don't know about."

He chuckled. "I do miss it all. But I love you. I want to be around for you and the baby. I just need to figure out how to balance every-thing out." He tapped the side of his head with his knuckles. "Up here, more than anywhere else."

"Okay, then tell me more about what you miss," I encouraged, wanting to know more. "What you loved about doing four people's jobs."

Axel scrubbed his hands over his face. "I don't know. I can't really put it into words."

"Well, why did you want to be successful in the first place? Do you remember?"

Surely there was a reason for his drive?

"What do you mean?" he asked, frowning at me. "Everyone wants to be successful in business."

"Yeah, I know. But you're so driven. More than anyone I've ever met. And it's not like you had a wife or a baby to care for, like my dad. So, what made you so determined?" I asked, pushing him towards a resolution for which he may not know the answer. "You know. What was the real reason you wanted to work so hard?"

"For you. For the baby," he snapped at me, seeming frustrated now.

I put my hands up. "I'm not accusing you of anything, honey. You're amazing, in every way. But if you want me to help you, then please, talk it out with me."

He sighed. "Okay. What do you mean?"

"I mean… what drove you? Back then, especially? What made you come out of graduate school and build an empire? Surely, that takes a special sort of person."

He shrugged, like he didn't know.

"If you don't want to talk about it, that's totally fine." I said, grinning at him. "I'm happy to discuss the wedding or something else."

We'd decided not to call my parents and tell them about the engagement. Mom was finally stable and settled, and Dad was stressed at work.

We'd tell them when we returned home, which was more personal than on the phone.

I extended my arm and stared down at my hand. "I love my ring so much."

It was so large, it was almost gawdy. But the pink diamonds surrounding the white diamond in the middle made it so happy and bright. I was filled with glee every time I looked at it.

"I'm glad," Axel said, though his voice was soft, thoughtful.

I glanced back up. "Do you want to talk about it now?"

He met my gaze with an intensity that surprised me, then nodded.

"Okay. So, tell me. What was it?"

Axel crossed his arms over his chest and leaned back in his chair. "I needed to be a success."

"Says, who?" I asked.

"Says me. My parents."

"Your parents? What do they have to do with it?" I pushed. Now we were getting somewhere.

He glanced away and gestured to a waiter, who hurried over. "Yes, sir?"

"I need another coffee," he said. "Cappuccino, please."

The waiter looked my way, and I shook my head. "I'm fine. Thank you."

Once the waiter left, I glanced back at Axel. "Go on." I wasn't going to let the ordering of coffee distract me.

This was annoying him, had been for a while. And now that he finally wanted to talk to me about it, I wasn't going to let him slip away.

"You were talking about your parents."

He sighed, shifting in his chair. "My parents are wealthy. Old money. They paid for my education—boarding schools and Ivy

League—but made it clear that they wouldn't support me afterward. Not that I would have ever asked them to, but they drilled it into me from a very young age that once I graduated, I was on my own."

He exhaled slowly, sounding almost relieved at the confession.

"I suppose that's normal," I said, shrugging. "Most parents want their kids to stand on their own two feet after college. I know mine did."

"Yeah, but yours would have helped you if you needed it. Let you go home to stay with them while you found a job, or at least made you feel like they wanted you to succeed."

"They didn't want you to succeed?" I repeated. "You really think that?"

He looked at me like he couldn't believe he'd just said it. "Ah, yeah. I uh…"

"You don't know? Don't remember?"

"They… I don't know."

"You do," I pushed. "You think they set you out in the world, well-armed with a good education, but you think they wanted you to fail, don't you? And with them wanting you to fail, they cut you off completely, didn't they?"

He nodded. "Ah, yeah. They… yeah."

I was putting it together now, slowly. But it was becoming clearer. "So, your absentee parents paid for school then cut you off, expecting you to fail, and what? Come home to them? Admit defeat?"

Pain crossed his features. "They never said anything, but I got that impression from time to time. Yeah."

I sat forward, my lower back aching. "So, you're twenty-three, twenty-four, broke, and needing a job. What do you do?"

Axle glanced away. "I bunked in with a friend and his parents, and got a job. Fast. Developed my own clients, went out on my own, found Cheryl, and the rest is history."

I rubbed my belly, the baby kicking out under my ribs. "And when along that road did you think to yourself, 'I'm gonna show them I can succeed on my own, and I'm never going to ask them for help?'"

Because that made perfect sense. That a guy who had been cut off, kicked out, and left to fend for himself had decided to beat all expectations and work harder than anyone had ever imagined.

"I didn't decide," Axel said, blinking rapidly.

"I kinda think you did," I told him. "Maybe not in those exact words. But I suspect your drive to succeed comes from your parents, indirectly."

He shuddered. "I hate to think that. I don't want them to be the reason for my success."

"They aren't." I shook my head. "You are the reason you're successful. Your hard work. But maybe it's time to look at whether it still makes you happy. Or even just sit back and look at what you've achieved. You don't need to prove anything to anyone anymore. Least of all, them."

They sounded like assholes.

"I need to think about it," Axel said.

I nodded at him. "Sure. It's only a theory. I could be wrong."

Axel drank his coffee, deep in thought, and I ate the rest of my fruit. I didn't bring up the topic again and tried not to be offended by the fact he withdrew and didn't talk to me for a while after that.

He was thinking about why he was so driven, and how closely knit his success was to his parents' behavior, when he'd probably thought they were completely separate issues.

We left early for the airport, arrived with time to spare, and were soon on our way home again.

This time, as an engaged couple.

Chapter 16

Axel

WE FLEW HOME, GOT PICKED UP BY ONE OF THE DRIVERS, THEN WENT back to our new house. I tried to chat with Chastity while we traveled, but even I knew I was distant. I couldn't help it. My head was in a downward spiral the whole time, trying to make sense of our last conversation.

The denial was huge. Everything inside of me screamed she was wrong. I didn't want to even consider the fact that some of my success might have *anything* to do with my parents.

My horrible, narcissistic, totally abandoned me and made me feel unwanted my whole life, parents.

They couldn't be my driving force to succeed. They couldn't be. The very idea sullied the best part of my life, outside of Chastity and our little one.

My newly engaged fiancé went straight to our bedroom to have a nap as soon as we'd dropped our bags by the front door.

I needed to distract myself, so I went to the office and logged onto the computer, feeling a sense of calm fall over me with the familiarity of the move. I checked emails and got straight back to work.

I was pleasantly surprised to read the day's report from Patrick and Cheryl. Everything was totally under control, but they wanted my help with something they couldn't do themselves.

That's what I wanted to hear. That I was needed at my own company. Finally.

After a quick dinner, we headed into the hospital for a quick visit to Chastity's mom.

Katherine had a private room on the third floor, and as soon as we reached the door, Chastity cried out, "Mom!" and rushed to her side.

Chastity leaned over to hug her mother, both of them groaning with the effort. Their swollen bellies made the task strangely jigsaw-like, the pieces just not fitting into place the way the owners wanted them to.

"How was your vacation?" Katherine asked, a smile on her face as she perused her daughter. Then she grabbed Chastity's left hand, her eyes bulging out of her head. "Is that what I think it is?"

Chastity glanced over at me, her eyes lit with happiness. "Yes. Axel proposed on the trip, and I wanted to tell you and Dad in person."

Katherine let go of Chastity's hand and rubbed the sides of her belly. "Congratulations. Both of you. You look very happy."

I walked up and stood next to Chastity. "We are. Thank you, Katherine. But how are you? That's why we're here, after all."

Katherine swatted her hand through the air dismissively. "Oh, don't worry about me. I have a hundred doctors and nurses fluffing around to make sure I stay on my ass and don't move. At this rate, I'll be three hundred pounds by the time I deliver."

Chastity ran her hand over her mother's shoulder. "Actually, Mom, you look like you've lost weight."

And she did. There was no way she was putting on weight, even with the lack of exercise.

"It's the medication. It keeps the fluid down. I'd gotten really puffy." Katherine patted her cheeks.

Chastity and I exchanged worried looks. Katherine didn't look well.

I moved over to a chair on the other side of the room and sat down while Chastity sat right next to her mom. Two women. Two big bellies. They were a beautiful sight, really, though it was quite unusual to have a mother and daughter pregnant simultaneously.

"We should have organized a photo shoot for you two," I said, off the cuff. "Both pregnant at the same time."

Chastity laughed and glanced at Katherine. "Oh, yeah. Imagine that."

Katherine blinked at me. "I don't think I have any photos of this pregnancy. None. I had a ton of me when I was pregnant with Chastity."

I pulled out my phone and held it up. "Do you want one now? I can snap a few pictures. Or I can arrange a photographer. They can come here if you want."

Katherine pulled back the blankets and slowly moved her legs to the side of the bed. "Now. Here. In front of that plant in the corner," she said, pointing over near the window.

"Okay," Chastity agreed as they both stood and waddled over to the only green thing in the room.

"I like this color on you," Katherine said to Chastity, motioning to her new pink dress.

"Thanks, Mom." Chastity glanced at me with a grateful smile. I'd encouraged her to buy a few new things while we'd been away. I'd been shocked to know that she hadn't bought enough clothes for herself through her pregnancy, not wanting to spend the money.

They stood by the only non-hospital looking wall, side by side, belly to belly, looking at me, smiling.

I lifted my phone and took a photo, then feeling creative I said, "Can you stand facing one another so we get the bellies?"

Chastity laughed but moved to turn towards her mother, grabbing the underside of her stomach to accentuate the curve.

Katherine flinched as though in pain but turned also, holding her belly tight. Even though Chastity was four weeks ahead of Katherine in gestation, Chastity's belly was smaller.

I wasn't sure how that was possible, but what did I know about pregnancies?

"Smile," I said, though Katherine was getting paler by the minute.

I snapped a few shots quickly, then rushed forward to grab onto her hand. "I think it's time to get back into bed."

She nodded and didn't fight me as I held her arm and helped her the few steps back to her bed.

That's when Pat walked in, his gaze narrowing immediately. "What happened?"

"I don't know," I told him as he rushed forward to flick back the blankets for her. "She stood up to have a photo with Chastity, then went pale."

He pressed the call button for the nurse and began fussing over Katherine as she climbed back onto the hospital bed. "You know you're not supposed to get up."

She sighed. "I still go to the toilet and shower myself, you know."

But from the looks of it, she may not even be doing that much longer. She was as pale as the sheets surrounding her.

The nurse came in and we gave her the short story of what happened.

"Let me check your blood pressure," the nurse said, then shook her head. "Your blood pressure is too low."

"Yeah, those stupid meds are working too well," Katherine grumbled. "Pre-eclampsia is supposed to have me fainting from high blood pressure, not the other way around."

The nurse made a note in her chart. "I'm going to talk to the doctor. Will be back as soon as I can." She excused herself and left.

Patrick sighed and visibly shook himself. "Okay... so, how are you two? How was the vacation?"

"Amazing," Chastity said, then stepped forward, arm extended and wiggling her fingers. "And look."

Patrick took her hand and stared down at the ring I'd chosen for his daughter.

He glanced my way. "Congratulations." He stuck his hand out.

I shook it and mumbled, "Thanks." Happiness spread through me.

Technically, I probably should have asked Pat's permission, again. But he'd given me the green light months ago, I'd just been waiting for the right time.

And the right time being the time I thought she might say yes.

"Do you have a wedding date?" he asked, sitting down on one side of Katherine's bed, while Chastity sat down on the opposite side.

I glanced at my fiancé, who shrugged. "No idea. I'm just enjoying the moment and being engaged. It's awesome."

She happily rubbed her belly and I just stared at her. She was truly the most beautiful woman I'd ever seen in my life.

"We haven't talked about it, but I'd like to get married as soon as possible. So, it really depends on if you want a maternity wedding dress or not."

Chastity stared at me, then blinked a few times in rapid succession. "You want to get married in the next four weeks?"

I grinned and thrust my hands into my pockets. "I'd marry you tomorrow, if you'd let me."

I heard Katherine's groan and glanced up. She was shaking her head. "Seriously. These two are nauseating."

I laughed, how could I not. "I'm sure you two are just as bad in private."

Katherine and Pat glanced at each other, and for the first time, I saw a spark of something I'd never seen before. A deep love. An understanding. Gratitude.

I stepped closer to Chastity and took her hand when she reached for me. "So?" I asked. "What do you say?"

"What do I say to what?"

"Getting married sooner rather than later."

Her eyes widened. "You were serious?"

"Of course, I was. But I totally understand if you want to wait until after the babies born."

Chastity's eyes sparkled as she grinned at me. "She'd be cute as a flower girl."

"She would," I agreed, though the idea of waiting years to marry the woman I loved felt like a kick to the gut.

I bent forward to kiss her fingers, then moved back to my chair.

"You okay?" she called out to me.

I nodded and forced myself to wipe the disappointment off my face. I was absolutely bursting to tie myself to Chastity in every way possible, and yet she didn't seem worried at all.

Perhaps it was the age difference? To her, she probably thought she had all the time in the world.

For me, I felt like I'd waited my whole adult life—decades—to find her. I didn't want to wait a minute more to marry her.

"How's work been, Pat?" I asked. "Now that we're back, if you need time off…"

"No. It's fine for the moment." Patrick reached onto the bed and grabbed for Katherine's hand. "I think I'd drive Kaiti nuts if I was here all day."

"Oh, he would," she confirmed. "Believe me, he's worse than the doctors."

"Well, you're the most important thing in the world to me," Pat said, showing a rare insight into their relationship. "And I don't know what I'd do if something happened to you."

Instead of responding with her normal amount of cold wit, Katherine teared up, her eyes glistening with tears.

Everyone was quiet, and I looked at Chastity, who was tearing up too.

Oh, no.

"Well, I'll be back in the office tomorrow, so if you need to leave at any time, you can," I said, forcing the words into the uncomfortable silence.

Patrick looked my way, then grinned. "You're busting to get back to work, aren't you?"

I nodded. "Definitely."

"Did you at least take time off while you were away?"

"I did!" I told him proudly. "Ask Chastity. I barely opened my laptop."

"I don't believe it," he said, blinking at me.

"It's true," Chastity said. "I was totally spoiled. We had sleep ins and long lunches, and lots of shopping and drinks by the pool. Axel didn't work at all, really."

Pat laughed. "Well, good for you. But I know my best friend, and you'll be busting a gut to get in there tomorrow. You're the very definition of a workaholic, and I've always admired you for your drive."

I forced a smile to my face. "So, I'll see you tomorrow, bright and early."

"You will."

The conversation happily moved away from work, to the impending babies. I nodded and smiled when required, but Chastity mostly carried the conversation, so I had time to sit back and think.

I had been a workaholic for so long and loved every minute of it. Had I changed? Or was the true reason behind my drive to succeed that I wanted to prove my parents wrong? That I could do it on my own.

Because now that I had Chastity, I didn't feel like I had to prove anything to anyone. What did that mean for my future?

Chapter 17

Chastity

AXEL WANTED TO MARRY ME NOW? LIKE THIS? THIRTY-FIVE WEEKS pregnant, swollen and uncomfortable? Seriously? My head was spinning with the implications of what he'd said.

Where would we get married? What about flowers? A dress? A reception?

When the doctor came in to talk to Mom about her medication, I hugged her tightly and left with a promise to drop by the next day.

As soon as we were home, I couldn't hold the words in any longer. "Were you serious about getting married soon?"

He tucked the car keys on the hook by the front door and locked the door behind him. "Yeah, I was."

"But seriously?" How was that possible? Surely, he wanted to wait a few years, until I was finished breastfeeding and got my body back?

He pulled me gently into his arms. "I would marry you today. Tomorrow. Whenever you say the word. It's your choice if you want to wait until after the baby's born."

"But I'm a whale," I whined, sliding my arms up around his neck. "I won't fit into any dress."

He leaned forward and kissed my lips. "You are more beautiful now than ever. And I would be so proud to marry you, even nine months pregnant. I actually love the idea of it."

I frowned. "What do you mean?"

"I mean, the baby is the ultimate commitment to one another, and the wedding will celebrate that."

He was serious.

Suddenly I could see it. A long, long dress flowing over my bump, pink roses in my hair.

"How do you want to do it? Small? Big? Reception? No reception?"

He grinned at me. "I want, whatever you want. Money's no object, of course. Book anything, buy anything, I just want you to be happy."

I turned on the side to get my belly out of the way, then leaned against him to hug him. "Can I think about it?"

I wasn't sure I had the energy after all the renovations to plan an event like that.

He chuckled and kissed the top of my head. "Of course. There's no pressure. I just... thought it might be romantic, that's all."

I glanced up and he kissed my lips this time. "Thank you. I'll talk to my mother about it, I think." She'd probably think I was utterly crazy.

"I think that's a great idea. Give her something to plan and control from her hospital bed," Axel said, then kissed me once more to walk into the kitchen and grabbed two bottles of water from the fridge.

"That's another thing," I said. "Mom could be in hospital for months yet. I can't get married without her there."

Irrespective of the falling out we'd had, and any past baggage, I couldn't enjoy the biggest day of my life without her there cheering me on.

"That's true. Hadn't thought of that," Axel admitted, cracking open the bottle and taking a few chugs on the water. "Sorry. Wasn't thinking."

I shrugged. "It's all good. You want to marry me, that's all that's important."

"So true," he said, walking over to put his hands around my non-existent waist. "How about we go to bed, and I show you how much I love you?"

Heat unfurled inside my belly, shooting pleasure along my veins. "Yes, please."

"You're not too tired?"

"For you? Definitely not." I stepped back and took his hand, tugging him to the bedroom where he took me to the stars and back again.

THE NEXT DAY I WENT INTO THE HOSPITAL AFTER LUNCH TO DISCUSS MY ideas with my mother. I'd been online all morning looking at wedding dresses and venues. If anyone was going talk me out of this crazy plan, it was her.

"Hey, sweetie!" she greeted me as I knocked on the door frame, then entered. She was looking pale but otherwise well.

"Hi, Mom. How are you doing today?"

"Not bad," she said, then swallowed hard. "Thirty-one weeks today, so that's really good. The baby is getting bigger by the minute and the longer he or she stays in there, the better."

Mom rubbed her huge belly and shifted in the bed as though she was uncomfortable. "You're thirty-five weeks now, right?"

I nodded. "Yeah. Have a check-up with my specialist tomorrow, actually." I grabbed the yoga ball in the corner of the room and rolled it over to the bed, then sat on it with a groan. "This is great. I can see why people like to sit on them during labor."

"Yeah, they are," she agreed, then cocked her head to the side. "What's up? You look like you need to tell me something."

I laughed. She always knew.

One of the many reasons I stayed away and didn't visit her when I was in my first trimester. She would have known I had a secret from the moment I walked in the door.

"I've been considering Axel's proposal that we get married while I'm still pregnant, but there are so many things to consider and worry about, and I want your advice."

She pushed herself more upright, then settled with both hands on her belly. "What's there to worry about?"

"You, for one thing!" I said, gesturing to my sibling in her belly. "I need you there. I could never have my day without you, but what if you're still in hospital?"

Her smile was tight. "When were you planning on the event?"

"Well," I began, "I spoke to a wedding planner this morning who said she could throw something together in four weeks, which would make me thirty-nine weeks. I know that sounds crazy. If I got into labor that week, it could ruin everything."

The more I talked, the crazier it seemed. Babies came anytime, and they were considered full term at thirty-seven weeks. I could go into labor on the day of the wedding!

Mom cackled with laughter. "You don't do things by halves, do you, sweetheart?"

I frowned at her. "Why aren't you trying to talk me out of this? Don't you think it's insane?"

I'd been prepared for her frowns and disapproval, and even a scream here and there. But this happy look she had on her face? I was not prepared for that.

Maybe she hadn't heard me correctly?

"Mom, seriously. Do you think it's smart to throw some expensive party together the week before I'm due?"

"Well, you were ten days late, so you know you could go way over your due date, Chastity."

My mouth dropped open. "Over?"

"Yes. A normal gestation is considered anywhere between thirty-seven to forty-two weeks."

I groaned and leaned forward on the bed. "Oh my God. Forty-two weeks! Imagine that." I couldn't. Another seven weeks of this? Getting bigger every day? "I'd be the size of a house."

Mom laughed again. "To answer your question, I do think it's insanity, but everything about you and Axel is insane. The way you fell in love around your dad, your ages, you finishing school and all the other pressures. Your pregnancy, the house. Everything has been done at lightning speed and yet I've never seen you look so happy, and Patrick said he's never seen Axel so happy either. So, I think you should go with your instincts on this one, sweetheart. What's your heart telling you?"

Tears swam in my eyes and my throat tightened with emotion and heat. "Um… that getting married heavily pregnant would be amazing. A sign of how much we love each other. The commitment we have to be a family."

It was so old-school, in lots of ways. With a marriage, you could marry someone, then divorce them and never see them again. But once you had a child together, you had to see that person for at least the first eighteen years of the child's life.

Nothing said commitment like a baby.

"Then do it!" she said. "Risk it. If you have to cancel due to the baby or a complication, who cares? It's not like Axel can't afford the cost."

"Mom!" I frowned at her.

"It's true!" she said. "He won't care, and everything can just be postponed to a month or so afterwards."

Excitement began to creep into my belly, then reality hit me hard. "But what about you? You could still be in here, in four weeks' time. I can't get married without you there, holding my hand."

Mom's eyes filled with tears, but she blinked them away as she reached for my hand. "I'll be there, sweetheart. And, although he may not be able to attend in person, your little brother will be there too."

"What?!" I croaked. "You're having a boy? I thought you didn't know?"

Mom hiccupped out a laugh, then swiped at the tears that ran down her face. "We weren't going to, but we've had so many scans now that it was becoming very obvious."

She grinned at me, and I lifted my hand then pressed my palm against the roundness of her belly. "My little brother. I can't believe it, Mom."

"Your dad is so happy," she said, her face now beaming with an infectious smile. Then she became serious, the tears welling once more. "I just hope he's healthy. The scans all say he's big and strong, but so much can go wrong now. Especially with my age. The doctors and nurses do nothing but refer to my age like it's a disease."

She tsked and I grinned up at her. "Ignore them. Your baby's a miracle. You just need to keep him in there a little longer."

She nodded, then squeezed my hand. "Show me what dresses you're looking at. Do you have any ideas what you want to do?"

"I do. I was thinking of something small and intimate, maybe fifty people. I found some hotels I like the look of, with great gardens for the wedding, and I did find a dress, but it is soooo expensive!"

She smiled, then brushed away another tear. "I'm sure Axel told you that you could have anything you like."

I nodded. "He did."

"And your father will want to help with the wedding or the honeymoon. I'm not sure, but he'll want to pay for something."

"Thanks, Mom." In the past I would have stressed about where Dad would get the money, whereas now I knew that Axel's company was paying him well, I tried not to worry.

I pulled out my phone and began searching for the photos I'd collected for this exact conversation. "Can I show you what I've found so far?"

"Definitely. Show me."

We spent the whole afternoon talking about wedding stuff. Dresses, flowers, reception packages and the wedding officiant. We laughed, we cried, and Mom even made some phone calls for me and booked the wedding planner so I didn't have to stress so much.

It was a total luxury, an un-necessary expense, but I couldn't imagine doing it all myself. Not at the scale I wanted, and not in four weeks.

By the time I left the hospital, I was desperately in need of a nap, but my heart was full to bursting. My mom was totally on board with me getting married in a month, and I would have a baby brother soon.

Life was good.

Now I just had to tell Axel and my dad the news!

Chapter 18

Axel

It was a bit of a surprise when Chastity told me she wanted to get married on September twenty-sixth, the week before the baby was born. But the shock soon wore off, and excitement set in. She would be my wife, and soon.

Within a few days, Chastity had met with a wedding planner she'd seen on Instagram, and the plans for our "special day" were underway. The hotel reception was booked, the officiant called, and Chastity was up to her eyeballs in magazines and notebooks full of quotes, dates and pictures of dresses and bridal bouquets.

The other amazing thing was that Katherine was still pregnant, still fighting the nurses, and holding onto her sanity—barely, according to Patrick. Despite their differences, Chastity's happiness was very much entwined with her parents' approval. Which brought me back to my job for the day.

I needed to call my parents. The wedding invitations had gone out, and I wanted to tell them myself before they received their silver and white envelope.

I picked up my cell phone once everyone else had left the office and hit the button to call them.

My mother picked up the phone. "Hello, Axel, this is a surprise."

Of course, it was. It wasn't Christmas or someone's birthday. "Hello, Mother, how are you?"

"I'm well, how are you?" she answered, her voice typically cold.

I forced a smile to my face so that my tone was pleasant. "I'm really good actually, and I wanted to share some news with you. Two pieces of news, actually." Now that I thought about it, I hadn't even told them I was going to be a father.

"Is Dad around? Can you put me on loudspeaker so he can hear me as well?"

"Very well. Give me a moment."

She seemed to put the cell phone down because there was a strange crackle, then the sound of her footsteps as she walked away. I waited. Then there were muffled voices in the background and the phone was picked up again.

"Hello, son," my father's big voice boomed through my cell phone.

"Hi, Dad. How are you?"

"Fine, thank you. How can we help you?"

I closed my eyes for a moment, anger simmering in my gut. I got friendlier, more personal service at the restaurants I frequented.

Just tell them and hang up.

"I wanted to share some great news with you both. I'm getting married."

There was a soft gasp at the other end of the phone. "To whom?" my mother asked.

"Her name is Chastity, she's the daughter of one of my oldest friends. We met last year and she's definitely the one." I nodded to myself as the un-rehearsed words just popped out. That sounded right. Good.

The was a long pause on the other end of the line.

"You two still there?"

"Yes. We're here," my father said.

"Congratulations," Mother said, her tone of voice high and pitchy. "When's the big day?"

"Well, assuming things go to plan, about three weeks."

"Three weeks? What's the rush?" she asked.

Not that it was any of her business.

"I want to be married to her as soon as possible, that's the rush," I snapped back. "She preferred to wait until after the baby is born, but I want her as my wife as soon as yesterday."

"The baby?" Mother squeaked.

"Yes. She's pregnant. Due in October." With a baby girl that is going to have her daddy wrapped around her little finger in no time, I was sure of it.

More silence.

For fuck's sake.

"Well, I just wanted to let you both know before the invitation hits your house. So, yeah."

My parents were still mute. What was going on in the background, I had no idea, but anger was beginning to build from deep within my belly.

They were being told that their only son was happy, getting married, and finally at the age of forty-three, becoming a father.

I pinched the bridge of my nose, knowing that I should hang up the phone and not delve into my childhood, but the need to get some answers outweighed my common sense. "Hey, do either of you remember why I wanted to run a company? Did I always want to be rich?"

Because I was, although I hated the word when I talked to most people, when it came to my parents, it was an easy descriptor.

Mom groaned. "No need to be so crude about money, Axel."

It also served to annoy them, which was always a bonus.

My father coughed to clear his throat. "You wanted to own your own business because I always did. You also grew up in a wealthy household. Why wouldn't you want to have the same things as an adult?"

"I suppose you're right," I gritted out. "So as far as you're concerned, I'm just copying you, Father. Is that right?"

The very idea galled me. As if I owned a company because my father did. He wasn't my hero, nor someone I aspired to be.

"Not copying, no," he replied, his tone haughty. "Why does it sound like you're provoking an argument, Axel?"

"I'm not," I declared, even though I could feel in the pit of my stomach that I was. I just couldn't help myself. "I've just been wondering lately why I still work so hard. After all, it isn't necessary."

I stopped for a moment, chewing on the thought, but my parents didn't speak, so I continued my monologue, "I think it's because you two refused to help me, kicked me out after college, and made me practically homeless. Despite your wealth, you decided I needed to do it all on my own."

It was coming together in my mind the more I thought about it. They'd barely been parents when I needed them as a child, then they'd gotten rid of me as soon as they physically could when I was grown.

"We paid for all of your education, including college," Mother defended. "That's the best foundation one can have in life. A good education, debt-free. You were much better off than any of your friends, even then. Now, look at you."

"Yes, look at me," I said, clenching my left hand into a fist where it lay on the desk in front of me. "A success in business, and now I'll have a wife and a daughter. What more could a man want? Right?"

Other than the respect and acceptance of his parents.

"You've done well, Axel," Mother said, her voice frosty despite the polite words. "We always knew you would."

Of course, they did. "Bet on the breeding, right?"

"Don't be crass, Axel." She didn't correct me, though. They took full credit for my success, which made me furious enough to throw my phone at the wall.

I took a deep breath, similar to those I'd heard Chastity practicing lately.

Calm. Stay calm. They're not worth it.

I'd had enough of this conversation. I was never going to get what I needed from my parents, so it was time to let go of the grudge I still held towards them and move on.

I had my own family now. No need to lament the loss of my old one.

"Thank you for my education," I told my parents. "But it's been twenty years now since you influenced any part of my life. I'm a success due to my own talent and perseverance."

"Axel—" Mother rushed in to say.

"Goodbye, Mother, Father."

"Axel!" Dad ground out, angry apparently. I didn't care.

I hung up.

There was a sting in my nose and throat that I chose to ignore, and when my phone vibrated with my parents calling back, I rejected their call and packed up to go home.

I arrived at my front door, not really remembering driving home. I shook myself. That wasn't safe. Shit. Maybe I should have called the driver?

Didn't matter now, I was home.

I took an extra moment before I walked inside, to just absorb where I was.

I didn't live in a bachelor pad anymore, with a revolving door for the women walking in or out. I didn't sleep alone every night, and I wasn't single. Far from it.

I lifted my hand and opened my door, calling out to my soon-to-be wife. "Honey, I'm home!"

"Hey! I'm in the kitchen! Did you eat? There's food in the fridge. I had some meals delivered today for us."

I walked into the kitchen and saw my gorgeous blonde angel sitting at the kitchen table that she now used as a wedding preparation station.

When she glanced up to smile at me, my heart ached, and my eyes filled with tears.

"Hey… you okay?" she asked, frowning at me.

I gulped and nodded, blinking the emotions away. "Yeah."

She pushed herself to her feet and flicked out her black dress that clung to her baby bump. "You don't look okay."

Then she did something perfect. She walked over to me and put her arms around my waist and pressed her head into my chest, hugging me tightly.

I put my arms around her and rested my chin on her head, holding her close.

My heart was still pounding too hard, but with Chastity's arms around me, it began to slow, to even out. Peace fell over me.

I exhaled and sighed. This was my family. This was my home.

The past was gone, and if my parents didn't want to be part of my future, they didn't have to be. I had to stop trying to make them fit.

When Chastity pulled away, she didn't talk to me immediately. She went to the fridge and showed me the meals that had been delivered. Lasagna and other pasta dishes, chicken breasts with vegetable sides and a container of Beef Stroganoff.

I chose the chicken and veggies and she heated it up, plated it, and pushed it towards me on the island counter.

I sat on the stool and dug into the food, my empty stomach grateful for the meal.

Once I'd finished, Chastity pushed a beer across the counter, then said, "Talk."

I laughed. She'd done well to wait this long. "I spoke with my parents tonight and told them about the wedding and the baby."

Chastity's eyes bugged bigger. "You hadn't told them yet?"

I shrugged. "It wasn't intentional. I just… we don't really speak. We call for Christmas and birthdays, and that's about it."

She frowned and rubbed her huge belly. "Really? Wow. I can't even go a week without talking to my parents."

I grinned at her. "I know, but your parents love you, sweetheart."

She tilted her head at me. "You don't think your parents love you?"

I glanced down at the cold beer bottle pressed between my palms and took a drink.

Did I? "No, I don't."

She didn't come around the island or touch me, for which I was grateful. I needed a minute.

"Is there anything I can do for you, my love?"

I glanced up and stared at my whole world. "You're already doing it. You're giving me a family, sweetheart. I just need to rethink my whole life."

I huffed out a laugh and ran my fingers through my hair.

"What do you mean?"

"I mean… I think I've always worked the way I do to prove to them that I could do it. You know, succeed without their help. And then it became a habit… I don't know."

That was when Chastity came around and sat next to me. She didn't talk, she just leaned her head against my shoulder and sighed.

"I love you, and I know they're not exactly the right age to be your parents, but you know you can share mine. And my grandparents, and my aunts and uncles. If you want more of a family, I've got lots."

I chuckled and sighed. "Thank you. I appreciate the offer."

Chastity was more than enough for me, but I needed to talk to Pat and Cheryl. Maybe it was time for me to shift my work paradigm a bit. It didn't need to be the way I defined myself as a person, or a man.

I provided for my family, and I knew Chastity wanted me. My time. My help.

Maybe it was time to stop lying about trying to slow down, and actually do it.

Chapter 19

Chastity

THE WEDDING PLANNER WAS AMAZING. SHE TOOK ALL THE STRESS OFF me with the planning and did most of the correspondence via text. It was like having some awesome, knowledgeable best friend who sent me pictures of colors, flowers, table settings and invitation patterns.

My belly was still rather high, making it difficult to breathe, but the doctor said I was measuring right on schedule, so it was full steam ahead for the wedding plans. My back and hips ached a little, but with regular chiropractic adjustments and short walks around the block, I was managing the pain okay.

I found a wedding dress I loved at a reasonable price. It was simple in design, ivory, with lace trim around the bodice and flowed over my baby bump and down to the floor.

We were having the reception at an old hotel slightly out of the city, with period features, a huge garden, and an old-world charm that I simply loved. We just had to hope and pray that we made it.

Two weeks out from the wedding, I was thirty-seven weeks pregnant and sitting at the kitchen table when I got a phone call from my mom around nine am.

"Hey, Mom, I was just going to take a shower, but I'll be there soon."

I'd been visiting almost every day, just to break up her day and to keep her in the loop about all the wedding plans.

"You might be better to come in later with Axel," she said, sounding nervous.

"Why, what's up?"

"They're taking me into the OR soon."

I stood up, my hand shaking as I lifted my arm to rest my hand on my belly. "Why? What's wrong?"

"Nothing's actually wrong. Really. I've hit thirty-two weeks, and the baby is healthy enough to come out. My body isn't coping as well as they want anymore, so it's time. Don't worry. Everything will be fine."

Tears welled up in my eyes and I pressed my hand to my mouth so I wouldn't cry out. She was reassuring me that she would be fine, and she was the one about to go into surgery.

"Chastity?" Mom asked quietly. "Are you still there?"

I nodded and swiped at the tears that leaked down my face. "I'm here, Mom. Okay. Okay… we have to trust the doctors, I suppose. If they say you and the baby are better off, then, that's great!"

I swallowed hard, injecting some enthusiasm into my voice. "You'll have your baby by the end of the day!"

Was it really safe for the baby to come out at thirty-two weeks? It didn't seem long enough.

"Yes. God willing," she whispered, and I almost broke down again.

The tears flowed and my throat ached. "You'll be fine, Mom. The baby will be fine. Get Dad to call me when we can come visit, okay?"

"Okay. I think I have to hang up, they're here."

"Is Dad there for you?" I asked urgently, suddenly realizing he wasn't in the background of the phone call.

"He's here. He's getting ready with surgical scrubs."

Thank God. "I love you, Mom. I'll see you soon."

"Love you too, sweetheart. See you later." And she hung up.

I collapsed back onto the chair, tears flowing freely down my cheeks. I let myself cry for a minute, needing the release from all the stress and overwhelming nature of what was going on.

But once the sobs subsided, I walked to my bedroom for some tissues, blew my nose, washed my face in the ensuite basin, and went in search of my phone again.

Axel picked up after one ring. "I was just about to call you. How are you doing?"

The tingling in my nose started up again, but this time I pushed the feelings away. "I'm okay. Do you know what's happening with my mom?"

"I've been in meetings all morning, but just got a message from Cheryl that Pat had to run off to the hospital. Katherine's having the baby today, is that right?"

"Yes," I said, swallowing hard to push the sadness down again. "She's only thirty-two weeks, but the doctors said that they'll both be better off if the baby is delivered now."

"Well, let's hope they're right," Axel said.

I nodded, unable to speak. What if something happened to my mom? Or my brother? How would Dad ever recover?

"Sweetheart," Axel said, when I didn't re-join the conversation, "your mom has the best care around, but I know you'll be worrying non-stop until they're both okay. If you give me an hour, I'll pack up and come home to be with you."

I bit my lip. I wasn't sure us sitting at home freaking out together was the right thing to do either, plus, an hour was a long time to be alone before he got home.

"How about I message Harry and ask him to pick me up? I can meet you at the office."

"You want to come here?" he asked, his shock obvious now.

I put my hand on my hip. "Are you embarrassed by your big, fat fiancé?"

He laughed. "You're gorgeous! I thought last night would have proven to you how beautiful I think you are."

Heat flushed into my cheeks at the mention of last night. Axel had licked my pussy until I'd come over him, then made love to me slowly until we'd both finished together.

I was getting big and awkward, but it wasn't stopping Axel's bedroom attention. If anything, he was making me lazy, doing everything for me.

"Yes, you did." I grinned, even though he couldn't see me. "So, is it okay if I come to you? I might even get Harry to drive me to a baby store so I can buy a gift for the baby. I haven't gotten anything yet because I thought we had more time."

And now that I knew they were having a boy, I could buy some awesome little blue things. Our nursery was nothing but pink, from the curtains to the blankets, to the toys and the rug. It was absolutely pink perfection.

"That sounds like a great plan," Axel agreed. "Go shopping, then head over to the office when you're done. But if things change and you need to go to the hospital, message me, and I'll meet you there."

"Thanks, hon. I love you."

"I love you too."

I hung up to let Axel go, because more than likely he was now run off his feet at work. My dad was his main manager and had left work with no notice.

I took a settling breath and texted Harry. Luckily, he was actually out running an errand, so would only be ten minutes. I took that time to pack some food and bottles of water into my new bag and was waiting for Harry when he arrived.

"Where would you like to go first?" he asked as he opened the car door for me.

"Well, I'm not sure what it's called, but there's a little baby boutique on the same street as the hospital. Down near the intersection."

He nodded. "I know the one. Let's go."

I got in the car, and Harry drove us into town. I clutched my cell phone in my hands and checked the volume was set on loud three times.

"Everything okay?" he asked suddenly.

I burst out with a nervous laugh. Harry didn't make conversation often, even when I tried to engage, so him asking a question out of the blue about me made me feel like I was being too obvious with my anxiety.

"Oh, ah. Yes. Thanks for asking."

Harry went back to being quiet, and I suddenly needed to talk to someone. "My mom was just taken in for her C-section, and she's only thirty-two weeks, so I'm a little worried for her and the baby."

"That's understandable," Harry said. "Is that why you want to go shopping? For your new sibling."

I grinned at Harry, still clinging to my cell and praying for a message from my dad to say everything was okay.

"Yes. Exactly. And hopefully by the time I've found something for the baby, my father will have messaged me to say they're out of surgery."

"I hope that happens," Harry said, and we lapsed back into silence.

As luck would have it, things worked out exactly how I'd hoped. I was paying for my baby brother's gift when my phone rang loudly.

"Oh, oh. Here. I've gotta answer this." I shoved my credit card at the woman behind the counter who'd heard the whole story over the half hour I'd been shopping and answered the call.

"Hey, Dad! Is everything okay?"

"Yes. Your mom's fine, the baby's fine. You have a new baby brother."

My hand flew up to my mouth, the knot in my stomach that had been making me feel sick for the past hour releasing in a flash.

"Oh, Dad, that's so amazing. How's the baby? How big is he?"

"He weighs almost four pounds and he's doing very well. They've taken him straight to the NICU in case he gets jaundice, but the doctors said that he should only be in there for a few days, hopefully. But he's safe."

I held my breath and was almost afraid to ask, "What about Mom?"

"She's okay," Dad said, but it didn't sound like it.

"What happened?"

"Well, her blood pressure skyrocketed in surgery, and she lost a lot of blood. She's still in there. I had to come out with the baby."

I pressed my lips together, hard. "Um…"

"She'll be okay. We just have to wait for her to come out of surgery."

"I'm just down the street," I told him, taking back my credit card and gathering the bag with all the baby's goodies in it, "How about I come straight to the hospital now?"

"Thank you," I whispered to the woman who'd helped me in the boutique, and she waved me off with a big smile.

"If you want to," Dad said.

"Yes. I do."

"I don't want you to be stressed, Chastity."

I walked out of the shop, rolling my eyes heavenward. "Dad. I'm going to be worried about Mom no matter what. I'd rather sit with you than worry at home."

"Okay. See you soon." We hung up.

Harry opened the door for me. "Jump in. I'll drive you down to the hospital."

I considered walking the two blocks, but my nerves got the best of me. "Thanks, Harry."

I sent Axel a message in the car.

The baby is here! A little boy, almost 4lbs, and healthy. Mom is still in surgery, so I'm going to the hospital to sit with Dad. See you there when you can.

In the two minutes it took for Harry to drive me to the front of the hospital, Axel texted back.

Congratulations! That's great. I'll get out as soon as I can. See you at the hospital. Take care of yourself.

I grabbed the gift bags, thanked Harry, and rushed into the hospital.

I found my father on level three, in Mom's room. She wasn't back yet, but I put my arms up and hugged him. "Congratulations, Dad. You have a son."

He pulled back and smiled at me. "And he's amazing. Do you want to see him?"

I gaped at him. "Can I?"

I put the gift bags down and tucked my cell phone into the pocket of my pregnancy leggings.

"You need to wear some special gear, but you definitely can. We can go now if you like?"

I nodded and walked with dad towards the door. "Have you heard any more on Mom?"

He shook his head, lines creasing around his eyes, showing his worry. "No. But they said they'd tell me as soon as they have news."

I grabbed his arm, holding my huge belly with my other hand. "Let's go see my baby brother."

Chapter 20

Chastity

MY HEART ACHED AS I STARED THROUGH THE GLASS WINDOW OF THE special care nursery. I'd been told that the contact was limited to only my dad today, but I could come back in a few days to visit my brother.

He was so tiny, attached to monitors and oxygen. He was beautiful and perfect, but seeing him there filled me with fear.

I put my hand up on the window, the cold pressing into my palm. *Poor baby.*

My daughter kicked out at me inside my belly, and I rubbed the spot she'd made contact. "Your uncle made it out into the world before you, baby girl," I said, joking with her quietly. "He's going to be competitive, I can already tell."

My father stepped out of the nursery and shut the door behind him.

"He's so beautiful, Dad. Do you have a name yet?"

He turned to stare back into the room. "We've narrowed it down to a few, but your mom and I haven't agreed yet." He swallowed hard, his throat muscles working. "When she wakes up, we'll decide together."

I turned towards him and put my arms out, giving him a quick hug before he pulled back. He didn't really seem happy to have me here, but I wanted to be supportive.

"Maybe we should go back to Kaiti's room and wait," he suggested.

"Okay, Dad." I held my belly as I waddled down the hall and into the elevator, then headed back to her room.

It would be my turn soon, to be in this hospital, having our baby.

I shivered, then pushed away the fear that came with the thoughts of labor. I glanced across at my dad as we walked. He was really worried about my mother, more worried than I'd ever seen him about anything before.

"Chastity!"

I looked up and saw Axel sprinting along the corridor. "You're here. Thank God. I've been looking everywhere for you. I think your phone's off."

"Oh, no. The battery must have died," I said, tugging my cell out of my pocket. The screen was dead even when I pushed the buttons. "Shit. Sorry, honey, I didn't realize."

I kissed Axel quickly and smiled at him. "I'm okay. My brother is doing great, we're just waiting on the doctor to tell us how Mom's doing."

Axel smiled suddenly, then tugged on my hand to encourage us to follow him into Mom's hospital room. "Oh, haven't you heard? They came in before while I was waiting for you. Katherine's out of surgery and in recovery."

"How is she?" Dad asked, stepping closer and grabbing Axel's arm.

Axel didn't miss a beat. "They said she's doing well."

My father staggered sideways, and Axel grabbed hold of him then gently directed him back into a chair to sit down.

"You okay, Dad?" I asked, noting the paleness of his cheeks.

He nodded. "Yeah. Just... um... give me a minute."

Axel and I exchanged worried glances.

"How about I go get you a bottle of water, Dad? There's a vending machine down the hall."

"That's a great idea," Axel said, before my dad could protest. "Can you grab a few extra?"

"Definitely. Back in a few minutes."

I hurried down the hall and grabbed some water and a few snacks. I was getting a little nauseous, which meant I had to eat.

When I got back to the room, there was a nurse there, speaking to my father. I'd missed the conversation, obviously, but everyone was smiling, so that was a good sign.

The nurse left and I hurried up with the water and snacks. "What's going on?"

Dad turned to me. "Basically, Kaiti lost a lot of blood, and they had to put her under fully and operate on her further after the c-section."

My hand flew to my mouth. "Oh, God."

"She's okay though. They said it's a relatively common side effect. She'll be waking up in a few hours possibly, so they said we should go home, get some sleep and maybe come back tomorrow."

"Are you going to do that?" I asked Dad.

He laughed. "No way. But you two should. Go get some sleep and come back tomorrow when your mom is awake and feeling better."

I wasn't sure my mother would feel very well the day after major surgery, but I wanted to see her anyway.

"I'll be back in the morning, Dad." I gave him a quick hug.

Axel extended his arm for a handshake. "Congratulations again, Pat. I can't wait to meet him."

"And I can't wait my granddaughter," my father said with a big grin.

We left and went home, my heart heavy.

Axel and I ate an early dinner, and I had a long bath to relax before bed.

Just as I was beginning to get all prune-like, and was readying myself to get out of the tub, Axel walked in. "You okay in here?"

I chuckled and nodded. "Yeah, fine. Just relaxing."

And what else did I have to do? More nesting? Shopping? Planning. No. My wedding was officially screwed. And I didn't care, or I shouldn't care. What else should I have expected, wanting to get married with both my mom and I in our third trimester?

Axel put the lid down and sat on the toilet, then faced me. "You don't look relaxed. In fact, you look… angry."

I glanced away, trying to clear my features of the feelings coursing through me, but it was impossible.

"Talk to me. What's wrong?"

I groaned and pushed myself back in the bath, grateful for the huge, deep tub that allowed the water to cover all of me. "I'm not angry. Or I suppose I'm angry at myself for being so selfish. All I can think about at the moment is the fact that we have to cancel our wedding."

Even saying the words made me tear up, and I dashed them away.

"I should be just grateful that my mom and baby brother are here, and they're both going to be okay. And yet, I can't believe I'm admitting I'm actually upset we have to postpone our wedding. How stupid is that?"

"It's not stupid or selfish at all," Axel reassured me, his gaze filled with love and understanding. "Is it the first thing you thought of?"

I frowned at him. "Of course not. I didn't even think about the wedding until we got home."

He smiled at me. "Then don't be too hard on yourself. Your initial reaction was about your mother, you've just realized that today has a flow on effect the rest of our life."

I pouted now. "Yeah, I know."

"You're allowed to be disappointed, sweetheart. You've been planning the whole day, and looking forward to it, and so have I. Remember, your mom has been looking forward to it too. She'll be disappointed as well. But in the long run, it doesn't matter. If we have to postpone it for a few months…" He shrugged. "So be it."

I nodded, blinking quickly and sending more tears down my face.

So stupid.

"Hey, don't beat yourself up over this. You're almost thirty-six weeks pregnant and had a very stressful day."

He went down onto his knees, kneeling next to the tub. "Do you want to know how selfish my thoughts have been today?"

I nodded. Anything to help me feel better about myself would be great.

"I couldn't stop thinking about how lucky I was that you and the baby were healthy."

I rolled my eyes. "That's not selfish."

"It is when my best friend's wife is in the hospital and the baby's in the NICU. I was just so grateful that it wasn't you."

He looked so worried that I couldn't help it, I twisted around in the water with the grace of an elephant and kissed him. "I love you."

"And I love you too."

Axel helped me out of the bath, and we were soon wrapped up in each other, naked and quiet in our bed.

"I hope Mom and the baby are okay," I whispered into the dark.

"They will be," Axel said. "Katherine's strong, and that baby boy will have Pat's fire, I know it."

I squeezed him tighter, nuzzling into the nook of his shoulder where I was cuddled. "I'm so grateful for you, you know that?"

He kissed the top of my head. "Ditto. Now sleep, so in the morning you can go visit your new brother."

I didn't think I'd be able to sleep. Not with the shitty thoughts and constant worrying about my mother whirling around in my mind. But I did.

THE NEXT MORNING, I WENT INTO THE HOSPITAL AND AXEL WENT TO work.

My heart was in my throat when I walked into my mom's room, but I was greeted by a beautiful sight. My mother sitting up in bed, sipping on a cup of tea.

"Chastity."

"Oh, Mom. You look wonderful," I said, rushing to her side.

She was deathly pale, but there was a brightness in her eyes that I hadn't seen in a long time. "I feel a little strange but there's no pain, thanks to all the meds they have me on. How are you doing, sweetheart?"

"I'm good," I said, sitting in the chair next to her bed like I had every day for the past two weeks. "Your tummy is half gone and you look so good."

She shrugged. "I'm recovering well, so I'll be able to make your wedding in a few weeks."

I gaped at her. "Seriously? I was going to cancel it until you were recovered. Maybe next year some time?"

"No way," she said, shaking her head. "I'll be discharged soon enough, and the doctors have said the baby is doing really well. He's a real fighter. So, assuming he starts feeding properly and doesn't have jaundice, we'll both be home soon enough."

Tears burned in my eyes. "That's too much pressure on you, Mom. You don't need to—"

My mother put her hand out to stop whatever words were coming out of my mouth next. "I want to. Look… I know I haven't been a fan of Axel's. Right from the start, I know I was a bitch to him."

I glanced down at her hand resting on my arm and didn't say anything.

"But he's a good man, and he's good for you. I never thought I'd say this, but he deserves you, sweetheart. With all your beauty and sweetness and intelligence and heart, I wasn't sure you'd find the guy that completed you. But you have. And you both deserve to have the day you planned."

I swallowed hard. "I want you there. It wouldn't be my special day without you."

Glancing up, I found my mom smiling at me. "I'll be there, and God willing, so will your brother. Even if I have to roll in via wheelchair and carry him on me."

I put my hand out and grabbed hers. "Please don't let it come to that."

She laughed. "I'll be there, so don't cancel anything."

My baby kicked and rolled inside my belly. "It was crazy of me to even attempt a wedding this close to the end of my pregnancy, let alone yours."

"You'll be fine," she said. "And I can't wait to see you walking down the aisle on your father's arm."

I exhaled slowly. "Are you really sure? I already called the wedding planner to cancel everything, but she was tied up and hasn't gotten back to me yet."

"You're not canceling anything on account of me," Mom said once again.

"You're really, really sure?"

"Yes!"

My phone began to vibrate, and I glanced down to look at the screen. "It's the wedding planner."

"Well, tell her that's nothing's changed, then you can go see the baby."

I grinned at her. "What did you name him?"

She leaned back on her pillow. "Grayson Patrick."

I stood up with the phone still vibrating in my hand. "That's beautiful, Mom. I really like it."

"Good. Now answer the phone and go see him. He's beautiful."

"I will!" I walked away to take the call, my heart singing a song that only I could hear.

My mother was well, my brother was here, and my wedding was on. Two weeks and counting.

My daughter just had to stay put, and not make an early entrance like her uncle.

Chapter 21

Chastity

Two weeks after my mother gave birth to Grayson, our wedding day arrived. Still pregnant, our baby girl still giving my ribs a daily beating.

I woke up at the hotel where we were getting married, blinking my eyes awake. For a moment I was confused because I was along and the dark drapes weren't the ones we had in our house, then I realized where I was.

"Oh my God… we made it." I groaned as I rolled over, stretching my arms above my head before attempting to get out of bed.

It took a try or three, my belly making it difficult to get moving in the morning, but once I was on my feet, I waddled to the bathroom to pee and have a shower. I washed my hair and shaved under my arms, amazed we'd gotten this far. I'd stayed awake for hours last night, hands pressed against my belly, waiting for the tell-tale signs I was going into labor.

But I didn't. Instead, it was officially my wedding day, and I was still pregnant. Thirty-nine weeks today.

When I stepped out of the shower, I was grinning to myself, and happiness was pulsing through me with every beat of my heart. "Baby girl, thank you so much for waiting for us to have this day. I really, really appreciate it."

"Chastity? You awake yet?" my mother called out from my bedroom.

I pulled the robe over my body and tied the belt above my huge belly. "Yeah, Mom. Just in the bathroom."

I opened the door and walked out, finding her already dressed and smiling in the main room, baby Grayson in a tight wrap around her chest.

Mom and Dad were big into the attachment parenting idea, especially with a preemie. The constant heat and contact meant Grayson was thriving, already well above his birth weight.

Mom clapped her hands together. "I've ordered some room service, so breakfast should be here soon. Then the hairdresser and makeup artist will arrive. It's all systems go."

I sat down on the bed, envying her energy and flat tummy. "How come you're all bouncy already, Mom?"

She laughed. "Well, it is my only daughter's wedding day."

"Yeah, but you had major surgery a few weeks ago, and you look amazing!"

She smiled a secret type of smile. "Your dad's been looking after me at home, and I've been lucky with my recovery. I feel so much better than I did while I was pregnant, so even with the pain, my body is rebuilding."

She rubbed her hands over Grayson's back, the very picture of maternal bliss.

I sighed, leaning back on my hands to try and relieve some of the pressure under my ribs. "I can't wait for this baby to come out now. Last week I wasn't really feeling it, but today… I'm done."

My mother grinned at me. "You only need to make it through today, then my granddaughter can come out and meet us all."

Tears filled my eyes and I blinked them away. So many feelings today. "I'm so glad you're here."

"I wouldn't have missed it for anything."

There was a knock on the door and Mom's face lit up. She loved room service. "I'll go get that." She hustled off to get the breakfast cart.

I managed to get to my feet and decided it was time to get dressed. I had pretty underwear to put on, a silk dressing gown, and a lot of beautiful food to eat.

And that's how the morning went. Surrounded by food and mocktails, chatting women and beauty.

The makeup artist did my makeup exactly how I wanted it—heavy enough to look good with lots of photos, but natural enough so I looked like myself. Just a good version of myself.

The hairdresser dried then curled my hair using a wand, then arranged half of it on top of my head and left a lot flowing down my back. Axel loved my hair long, so I wanted to wear it partly out.

My wedding flowers were mostly roses, red and white, so the hairdresser threaded some white roses into my hair that looked both elegant and whimsical.

"Oh, you look beautiful, sweetheart," my mother said, looking at me from across the hotel room.

I glanced in the mirror one more time, pleased with how everything was turning out. "Thanks, Mom. So do you."

Her hair was blow dried straight and her makeup looked great, too.

"Time to put your dress on?" Mom asked. "Your dad and the photographer will be here soon."

"Oh, you're right," I said, glancing at the time.

I got to my feet gracelessly and gathered my dress up in my hand. "I might need your help to put it on, Mom."

"Oh, no problem." she said, placing a swaddled Grayson very gently in his portable bassinet.

I put the dressing gown on the bed and slipped the dress over my head, my mom helping to bring the fabric down over my belly, then started on the drawstrings at the back.

"I'm glad you got this type of closure. So much better than a zipper or buttons."

I chuckled. "Yeah, the dressmaker suggested it since we really didn't know how big I was going to get."

My mother finished tying me up and I turned towards the mirror.

"You look absolutely beautiful." She squeezed my hand.

"Thanks, Mom."

I took a deep breath, then exhaled slowly. "This is really exciting, but I feel very nervous."

She just grinned at me.

"What if he changes his mind?" I whispered and my mother cackled with laughter.

"Changes his mind? Then he'd be officially crazy, and you wouldn't want him anyway."

I didn't think that would be the case, but hopefully it was a moot point. "What's the time?" I asked.

She was saved from answering because Dad knocked, then walked in the room. "How's my family doing?"

Then he stopped and stared at me. "Nervous?"

I nodded. "A little, but more in a 'I hope he doesn't change his mind' kind of way. Not in an 'I think I want to cancel' sort of way."

I shuddered at the very idea.

"Oh, he's not changing his mind," my father said with a grin. "He just about kicked me down the aisle to come get you. He's waiting by the metaphorical alter, as we speak."

Mom handed me my bouquet and I squealed softly, unable to stop the jolt of excitement that pulsed through my belly.

"Let's go."

"Okay." Mom gathered the baby up and tucked him into the wrap she wore, holding him close and tight against her body.

As a small family, we walked out of the room, down the hall and out to the patio that led into the back gardens.

Axel had rented out the whole hotel for the weekend, so we had complete privacy and all our family and friends could stay the night.

I looked around, soaking in the grandeur and pure beauty of the gardens. A white carpet runner stretched before me, decorated with rose petals.

"I'll go find my seat and see you both at the front." Mom kissed me quickly on the cheek, then kissed Dad too.

"Bye, Mom. Thank you."

She disappeared around the side and Dad held out his elbow to me. "Shall we?"

I nodded and reached for his elbow with my left hand, my right gripping tightly to my bouquet. "Yes. Let's do it."

AXEL

Waiting for Chastity to walk down that aisle was one of the most exciting, terrifying, heart-stopping moments of my life.

My parents were sitting in front of me, in the first row. I'd greeted them when they'd arrived, and they said they were staying for the night. I was pleased they were here, but that was about as far as the feelings went.

It was Cheryl, whose eyes were shining with tears and love as she stared at me, who gave me the feeling that my true family was here, supporting me.

As the music began, everyone suddenly rose to their feet and turned to look down the aisle.

I stared also, my heart thundering in my chest as I stood next to the female celebrant that we'd hired.

The doors to the hotel opened and two people emerged, small in the distance.

A beautiful woman in white and her father beside her.

As they walked closer, the sheer perfection of Chastity's shining face hit me like a lightning bolt to my heart. The smile on her face and the love in her eyes were everything I'd ever dreamed of.

A woman to love, who loved me, and an eternity together.

My gaze dropped to the swell of her belly, tightly hugged by the flowing white material.

Our daughter.

She'd be here soon, and we'd be a family. One filled with laughter and playtime together and local schools. My children would never be shipped off to boarding school.

I smiled at my wife-to-be, a lump clogging my throat as she stepped even closer.

Pat dropped his arm then took her hand, lifting it for me to grasp.

I did, feeling the solid warmth of her fingers in mine, popping the dream-like quality of the vision and making it all the more amazing because it was real.

"Thank you, Pat."

"Thanks, Dad," Chastity whispered, then squeezed my hand and stepped up beside me.

One of her friends in a red dress stepped up from the front row and took Chastity's flowers away, then she turned towards me and held out both hands for me to hold.

I faced her square on, holding both of her hands in mine, ready to declare to the world and everyone around us that I would love her until the day I died.

The ceremony went quickly and before I knew it, it was time for the vows.

"The couple has written their own vows and would like to say them now."

Chastity smiled up at me, gripping my hands tightly. "Axel, I love you more than anything in this world. Thank you for the gift of our daughter, our house, and the life you're creating for us. I am grateful for you every single day. You make me so happy, and I know you're going to be the most amazing daddy to our little girl."

I had to look away as heat burned my eyes, but I pulled it together because it was my turn.

There wasn't a single sound around us, the quiet almost deafening.

I coughed to clear my throat, then laughed. "I should have gone first."

That broke the tension and the people around us laughed.

I blew out a breath and smiled at my woman. "Chastity, I adore you. Since the very first moment I met you, I knew you were special. Sunshine in a dark world. Truly beautiful when others only pretend to be. We've gone through so much together this year, but we are stronger for it. There's nothing that can beat us now. And I know you will be an amazing mother to our baby, and I cannot wait to spend the rest of my life loving you."

Two single tears slipped down Chastity's face, but she didn't wipe them away. Her lip quivered when she tried to smile.

The celebrant spoke next. "With the power vested in me by the state of Florida, I pronounce you two man and wife. You may kiss the bride."

I reached for Chastity's face, cupping her cheeks then leaning over her belly to kiss her gently.

In front of our whole world, her parents and mine, her friends and mine, we were finally married.

We turned towards the crowd of our people who cheered and jumped to their feet.

I turned to Chastity and grinned. "Now it's time to party."

Chapter 22

Chastity

THE WEDDING RECEPTION WENT THROUGH THE AFTERNOON AND WELL into the night. We had a few official photos around the old hotel, then jumped straight into the decadent food and drinks, dancing to the music the DJ played and fun for all.

It was hell on my feet, and even though I'd found the most perfect white, flat, comfortable shoes for the wedding, my feet and ankles still swelled.

But all in all, a perfect day.

I finally met Axel's parents, who, to be honest, were as cold as ice. I would never have thought it was possible that they were the ones responsible for creating a man as warm, loving and amazing as Axel.

It blew me away.

I began getting cramps just after dinner but didn't let on to anyone. It wasn't much at first, just gentle tightening around my belly, similar to period cramps. Then, when it got too bad to keep up with the conversations around me, I just sat down and told everyone I couldn't dance anymore.

And luckily since I was thirty-nine weeks pregnant and the bride, no one questioned me.

We had a few short speeches and cut the exquisite wedding cake

I'd had designed by a local baker. Four layers of chocolate cake that was truly to die for.

Then the drinking and partying really began, at least for my guests who weren't fighting back the panic taking them over. If I was in labor, what should I do? Leave my own wedding? I couldn't do that.

Mom came and sat with me for a while, and although I tried, it became impossible to hide the pain rippling through me.

"Oh…" I gripped my belly and held my breath through the pain, then when I realized what I was doing, forced myself to exhale.

I'd read so many books on natural birthing, hypnobirthing, and theories that promoted a woman's power and right to give birth the way she wanted to. Which for me, was as naturally as possible.

But it was my mother who'd told me that the pain is like a wave. She said that it would swell up, be crazy intense, then drop away and disappear. She'd told me to ride the wave and not fight it, but fuck, that wasn't easy to do!

"Hey. Are you okay?" Mom asked, turning towards me.

I nodded, feeling the pain wave begin to subside and within thirty seconds, it was like it had never been. I sighed with relief then rubbed one side of my bump where the pain was particularly bad. "Yeah, just getting some cramping. It's probably all the dancing."

I rubbed my whole belly now and relaxed into my chair. *God, that's better…*

She gave me the side-eye. "How long has this been going on?"

I shrugged. No point lying now. "Since dinner or a little after."

Mom checked her cell phone. "So, three hours or so?"

I nodded, feeling the tightening in my belly beginning again, a little gentler this time.

Her lips kicked up. "I think you're in labor."

My heart thumped a little faster. I'd been thinking it too for a couple of hours now but had been trying to ignore it. Hearing someone else say it aloud made the possibility so much more real.

"I was hoping it was just Braxton Hicks," I said, rubbing the hardening flesh of my belly. It was like a drum again. Damn.

Mom nodded. "Well, most first labors take about twelve hours from start to finish, so there's no need to rush to the hospital. You just enjoy the rest of your party, and if you need to leave because it all becomes too much, tell me, and I'll smuggle you back to your room for a bath."

"A bath?" I repeated.

Mom nodded. "Or a shower. The hot water is great for pain relief. I spent most of your labor in a shower."

"Okay." Sounded odd to me, but what did I know?

Mom reached out a hand and squeezed my arm. "Just remember what I said. Don't fight the pain, it's doing something amazing. Functional. And make sure you rest in between every contraction. You'll need your strength for the last hour. Labor is a marathon, not a sprint."

Another cramp hit me, and I closed my eyes, visualizing the wave going up, going up, going up, BREATHE. Then all of a sudden it was falling away, and it was gone.

I opened my eyes and grinned at her. "Yep. I can do this."

"Of course, you can." She smiled at me. "You're one of the strongest people I know, and I'm so proud of you."

The words were unexpected and brought a smile to my face. "Thanks, Mom. I love you too."

Another pain hit and I worked my way through it.

I managed another hour before Axel dropped by to see how I was, and I couldn't hide it anymore. In fact, I didn't want to.

"Hey, beautiful. How are you doing?"

I stared up at him, admiring how gorgeous he looked, slightly sweaty and smiling brightly. "We... I think I'm in labor."

Axel stared down at me, his eyes wide and terrified. "W-what?"

"She's definitely in labor," my mother agreed. "Contractions are every five to seven minutes. A bit irregular still, but they're getting stronger."

Axel hurried around the table and sat down next to me. "Why didn't you tell me earlier?"

I shrugged. There was no rush.

"Because I didn't want to leave yet. The first stages of labor can take hours." And hours and hours. "Plus, if it's a false start, we would have left our own wedding for nothing."

Axel reached for my hand. "Let's go now then. Is it straight to the hospital? Or?"

"No. We have to call the doctor's service first to let them know we need the doctor to meet us there. Plus, Dr. Martinez said to stay at home until I can't stand it anymore." The last piece of advice she gave me at my thirty-eight-week appointment last week.

"So, what do we do?"

I didn't really know. Pain hit me and I bent forward, closing my eyes and gripping my belly, focusing on the wave but finding it difficult now.

"You could try a shower," Mom suggested. "Back at your room. Or maybe the hospital is the right place to be. Wherever you think you'll be more comfortable."

I blew out my breath. Where was my hospital bag? "Um… I think I want to go to the hospital." I'd feel so much better once I was there, I was sure. "But I left my bag at home."

It was filled with my clothes and toiletries, pads and baby clothes, and a hundred other little tips and tricks I'd taken off Instagram.

"I'll get your father to get that for you. I've gotta look after the baby. Hang on." Mom darted off to find Dad.

I shared a look with Axel, pain tightening in my back. "Not the way we planned to spend our wedding night, is it?"

Axel gripped my hand and I squeezed back, finding some relief from the pain.

"Watching you bring our first child into the world?" Axel asked. "Sounds like you've turned the best day of my life into the best night of my life, too."

"First child, huh?" I repeated, shifting on the seat to find a comfortable position. Everything was aching now. My back, my legs, my belly. "How many are we having?"

He laughed. "Now probably isn't the time to have that conversation. But I was an only child and I'd hope we'd have at least two, so they have each other."

I nodded, enjoying the relief in between contractions. "I always wanted three." *Or four.* But I wasn't saying that at the moment.

He smiled. "Sounds amazing."

I gasped as another pain hit me. Yep. I wanted to go to the hospital. Screw the shower.

"I wanna go," I said, launching myself to my feet.

That's when my water broke.

"Oh crap," I whispered as fluid gushed between my legs. "That's really gross." And it was. What a weird feeling.

Mom came back with Dad, who had his car keys in hand. "Where's your hospital bag? I'll go get it and meet you there."

"In our room," I said. "Next to the bed. It's a pink suitcase."

I glanced at my mother. "My water just broke."

Her smile was massive now. "Time for the hospital."

Axel was freaking out, I could tell, because he wasn't speaking, but he was kind of vibrating.

"Axel?"

"Yes!" he almost shouted. "Yes… car."

Dad swung his keys around his finger. "I'm off to your house. I know where the spare key is. See you at the hospital."

He slapped Axel on the shoulder. "Go, buddy."

I grabbed my phone and took my husband's hand, a little calmer now. "I think I want to get changed first. I'm a bit yucky."

"Oh, yes. Of course," he said, then put his hand in the small of my back and walked me slowly through the crowd and into the elevator.

A contraction hit me while we were going to our room, and I had to stop, press against the wall with my hands for a moment, and breathe deeply.

When it was over, I shook myself and kept waddling. I wanted my cotton dress that I'd packed for tomorrow. It was meant to be for our post-wedding breakfast, but that obviously wasn't going to happen.

I glanced at the man I now could legally call my husband. "Looks like everyone will be having the breakfast without us."

Axel chuckled nervously. "Yeah, I suppose."

We got to our room, and now I was calmer. Seeing Axel so freaked out made me immediately relax for some reason.

One of us had to be level-headed.

"What should I do?" Axel asked me.

"Untie my dress for me," I said, turning around and giving him instructions on how to loosen the dress.

Once it was free, it slithered off my arms and dropped to the floor.

I groaned with relief as my breasts were finally free. "Oh my God, that feels so much better."

Axel was staring at me like I'd gone insane. I had to tell him what to do, it seemed. "I'm going to have a really quick shower. You call Harry or whoever, and tell them we need a lift to the hospital. Just give me fifteen minutes."

That should be long enough.

"Okay." Axel took out his phone and started pressing buttons.

I managed to kick my shoes and underwear off as I waited for the water to warm then step under the shower.

It was bliss. My mother had been so right. Beneath the hot water the contractions felt so much more manageable.

"I've definitely gotta use the shower at the hospital if they let me." I called out to Axel. "This feels awesome."

Axel stuck his head into the shower, worry creasing his brow. "Are you okay if I quickly change clothes too?"

I nodded. "Of course. I'll stay in here a little longer."

I pulled the pins out of my hair, the dull headache I'd been holding all day ceasing as soon as my hair was finally free.

Next was my makeup. I scrubbed my face and washed all the grime away.

Four contractions later, I was clean and ready to get dressed.

I turned off the water and waddled into the bedroom. "It's so strange that when there are no contractions, the pain is gone."

Like it had never been there.

"That's good." Axel said. "Yeah?"

I nodded. "Yeah. Give me two minutes to get dressed then we can go."

I pulled on my cotton dress but didn't bother with underwear, pretty sure I was getting naked as soon as we got to the hospital.

A contraction hit and I bent in half, huffing and puffing through the wave until I could finally stand again.

Axel was there, a hand rubbing my lower back. "You okay?"

I nodded and straightened up. "Yep. Let's go before they get any worse."

They were getting stronger but were still relatively far apart. "Let's go, husband." I beamed up at Axel, who finally smiled properly back.

"Okay, wife. Let's go to the hospital."

"Let's go have our baby," I said, walking out of the room and towards the elevator once more. "It's strange to think I'm gonna waddle into the hospital like this and come out holding our daughter."

Axel kissed my lips as the elevator doors opened. "This really will be the best day of my life."

I blinked back the tears. "Mine, too."

We got in the car and headed towards the hospital, ready for our lives to change forever.

Chapter 23

Chastity

By the time we arrived, I could barely walk from the pain. The cramps were coming hard and fast, wrapping around my stomach and not letting go.

The tears had also started to flow. "I can't do this. I can't do this," I sobbed as I held tightly to Axel's arm.

"Do you want me to carry you?" he asked.

Panic set in. "God, no. I'm too heavy." And even if he could pick me up, what if he dropped me? No… just no. This wasn't some stupid comedy act. I was getting in there on my own two feet.

There was a short break, with the pain wave moving away. "It's stopped. Quick, let's go."

We staggered forward and made our way into the hospital.

Axel checked us in, and I was taken into a room and put on my back. "We're just going to check your cervix dilation, and then we'll understand more about how long you've got to go," said the nurse. "You'll feel some pressure."

Then she shoved her fingers up into my cervix and the pain was excruciating.

I screamed and she pulled her fingers out, but the pain was still pulsing inside of me.

"You're already seven centimeters. Well done."

"Well done," I groaned out. "She says well done."

"It won't be long now. I'll let the doctor know."

Not long? How long was not long?

"Can I have a shower?" I asked, launching myself up to sit where I'd been lying down.

"If you'd like to," the nurse said with a smile. "There are two shower heads so you can have one on your belly and one on your back if you need it."

"Thank you." I groaned, standing up and stripping straight out of my dress.

Another contraction came my way and I braced myself by grabbing onto the bed and breathing through the intense cramping gripping my belly.

As soon as it began to subside, I shuffled towards the shower and flicked on the taps. "Oh my God, no wonder women ask for an epidural."

I stepped beneath the shower and hit my lower back with the heat, sighing as the pain immediately decreased.

"Did you say you want an epidural?" Axel asked from the door. "Do you want me to call someone?"

I shook my head. "No. Seven centimeters is almost there. I can do this. Plus, I'm pretty sure there comes a point where it's too late anyway."

And that was the point I'd be asking for it, but that was okay. Less drugs, faster recovery, and less complications.

Fingers crossed!

"Oh, please."

Another wave hit me and this one hurt like hell. I cried out a little bit, whimpering as the panic that I'd felt walking from the car began to set in.

Then my stomach did something completely different, and I vomited in the shower. I retched and spat on the ground then turned the shower head towards the puddle to wash it all away.

"Oh my God, I am so sorry," I said to Axel, washing my mouth out with water. "That is not something you should see."

Axel's eyes were kind and full of love as he stared at me. "You're doing amazing, sweetheart. Keep going."

It only got harder from there. The pain got more and more intense until I couldn't stand anymore.

"I… I… need to lie down," I said, staggering back towards the bed, then the strangest sensation came over me. "No, I need to go to the toilet."

But I didn't want to sit on the toilet. What if I pushed the baby out? No.

The feeling was still there though, which was ridiculous but true. "I wanna go to the toilet."

"So, go," Axel said, indicating to the toilet.

I shook my head. "No. I can't."

I didn't want to sit on it.

Then another contraction hit me, and I cried out and dropped to my knees on the floor. Suddenly terrified, the pain overwhelmed me. There was no wave to ride anymore. There was only a wall of pain and darkness.

"Argh. Please make it stop. Please. I can't do this anymore."

"I'll get the doctor," Axel said, reaching out his hand to pull me up, but I shook my head, going onto my hands and knees and finding the position comforting somehow. My belly was dropped low, and I could relax my neck.

The door opened and people walked in. Who was there, I had no idea.

"I heard congratulations are in order," a woman's voice said. It sounded like Dr. Martinez.

"Ah, yes," Axel said. "We got married this afternoon."

Was it really still our wedding day?

"So, how are we doing Chastity?" the doctor asked just as a pain hit me.

I clawed the floor and cried out, so ridiculously grateful when it was over.

Axel's hand was in my hair, his voice in my ear. I wasn't sure what he was saying, but he was being supportive.

"How about we get you up on the bed so I can take a look at how far along you are."

I shook my head. No way.

"Come on, sweetheart," Axel said.

"No." I began to bear down, pushing back, then freaked out and stopped.

"Oh my God, I wanna push. Am I allowed to push?"

Was I allowed to? Wasn't there a rule about waiting until they said so? Was I dilated properly? Was I going to screw everything up?

The nurse was suddenly beside me on the floor. "Lift your legs, one at a time. I've gotta get this birthing mat under you."

I was shaking my head, but as she pushed at me, I did what she asked, letting them shove a thick, padded mat beneath me.

"What do I… Can I…" What did I do?

Axel was down on his knees beside me, his hand in my hair. "It's okay, sweetheart. The doctor is coming."

Where'd she go?

"You're doing so well, Chastity. So well. I love you so much," Axel murmured in my ear.

Dr Martinez's voice was behind me. "Chastity, you want to push, then push. When the contraction comes, bear down, slowly. Not one big push, just gently. Okay?"

I nodded, pressing my hands into the mat and pushing back.

When the next contraction hit, it was a relief to be able to do something with the pressure. I didn't have to just endure it, but I used the pain and pushed.

There was a shift inside of me. Flesh moving within me.

"Very good," the doctor said. "Take a breather for a minute. And do the same thing when the next contraction comes, just push a little more."

So, I did. When the pain swelled, I pushed back, feeling the twist of my daughter inside of me.

"I can see the head," I heard the doctor say from what seemed like very far away.

I couldn't help the guttural cries emanating from my throat now.

The ring of pain was a real thing. I wanted this over as quickly as possible.

One big push and my daughter twisted free.

I dropped my head, needing a minute. I couldn't open my eyes but there was movement around me.

"You're so amazing, sweetheart," Axel whispered in my ear. "Do you want to turn over and hold our daughter?"

I forced my eyes open and managed to roll over onto my back.

The doctor handed me my naked, blood-smeared little one.

I put her on my chest, still struggling to breathe, and looked down at her. She'd been crying when she was handed to me but as soon as she was set on my chest, she stopped crying and snuggled in.

"Wow." I whispered, putting both hands on her, cupping her tiny little head and running my fingers down her spine. "You're finally here."

"Let's get you up on the bed so you can both be comfortable," the doctor said. "We need to deliver the placenta, then you can stand up and move into bed."

That didn't sound pleasant, and it was strangely weird, but once done, I was beginning to buzz with a happiness I'd never felt before.

"How about you give the baby to Dad, and we get you up?"

The nurse put a pink, white and blue blanket over Axel's arms and she carefully picked up my baby and transferred her over to Axel.

His face filled with wonder and when he put his finger out to her little hand and she gripped it, his eyes filled with tears.

Love hit me so hard, I was left breathless. This was what it meant to be a family.

The nurse helped me up and I climbed into the hospital bed where they covered me in blankets and Axel came to sit beside me.

"Do you want her back?" he asked, not moving to give her to me.

I grinned at him, nestling into the pillows and sighing. "I've held her for nine months. I think it's your turn."

He chuckled and pulled her higher on his chest so he could kiss the top of her head.

The doctor did her final examinations and once they were sure I was in good health, nothing but some minor grazing, we were left alone.

"I'll be back to weigh and measure her," the nurse had said as she smiled and left the room.

I nodded, not worried in the slightest. It was the weirdest thing to go from feeling like you were going to die if the pain kept going and then all of a sudden, it was gone.

Like it had never even been.

"What do you want to call her?" I asked my husband, the man who'd turned my life inside out and back to front.

Who had changed every plan I'd made for myself, and re-made them with me a hundred times better.

He glanced up at me. "I thought we'd settled on Janie."

I grinned at him. "I agreed with that as part of the joke that after our parents had done such a good job with our weird names. But what do you really want to call her?"

"I always liked the name Margaret," he whispered, staring down at his tiny daughter, sleeping in her father's arms. "Maggie for short."

"Is that a family name?" I asked him. It was quite traditional, the opposite of our names.

"No. I just like it."

"Maggie," I repeated, staring down at her face.

Her eyes were closed now, and she had the most angelic little lips and mass of dark hair.

"Margaret Jane Patterson?" I asked with a grin.

He laughed. "Do you like any names you want to tell me?"

I shook my head. "I did, but now that she's here, none of the names I liked suit her."

And I loved names that could be shortened or changed for a person's age.

She could be Maggie, Mags, Margaret. Whatever she wanted. A queen's name for our little princess.

I glanced at the clock. Three am. "It's probably too early to call Mom and Dad."

Axel glanced at the time. "Your mother could be up feeding. Why don't you send them a text?"

It was a great idea, so I did, taking a photo of Axel with the baby and sending it to my mom.

"Baby's first photo," I said with a smile as I sent it off into the ether and closed my eyes. "I'm getting tired now."

"Then sleep, sweetheart. You did the most magnificent job, I'm so proud of you."

I forced my eyes open to see Axel staring back at me. "Who would have thought that this would happen? That a year ago when I saw you at the health club, we'd end up here?"

His smile was full of love and hope. "I would never have dared think it, but I dreamt of you. Of a woman with your heart, and I prayed that you would find me so I could love you."

The tears were happy ones now as I pulled myself up and he leaned forward to kiss me, our daughter, a piece of my heart, nestled between us.

Epilogue

Chastity

5 years later.

I CRADLED OUR NEWBORN SON IN MY ARMS, WATCHING HIM ROOT around, looking for a nipple to latch onto. He made the cutest little sounds, similar to a piglet, snorting and grunting away.

"Hang on a moment, little man. Give me a second." I moved my maternity top aside, unclipped my bra and put my hungry little bundle onto my breast.

I gasped a little at the ferociousness of his attachment, then sighed when the pain vanished as he began to drink.

Leo was only ten days old, so my nipples were still getting used to being fed on again, but he was doing amazing overall. Sleeping well, feeding well.

Motherhood was so much easier with my third. The pregnancy, the birth, everything had been easier. I was so much more relaxed this time and was finding myself enjoying Leo more because of how little I worried.

I'd kept my other two alive, I could do it again.

I heard a little shriek and looked up to see my eldest torturing her brother. I narrowed my gaze at the birthday girl and called out, "Maggie, share the trucks. You know they're his."

Maggie was a fiery little five-year-old and Thomas was my naughty little three-year-old. They were my whole world, even on the days they drove me insane.

Our children were the best thing I'd ever done, except maybe choose Axel as my husband. They came in a pretty close tie for first.

"Hey, beautiful," Axel said as he stepped out onto the back patio and kissed the top of my head. "How's your morning been?"

"Great. But the kids have been waiting for you to get home."

He slid into the lounge chair next to me quietly, since the two eldest hadn't spotted him yet. "For any particular reason? Or just because I'm the easy one?"

I grinned at him. "They want to go in the pool."

We'd had the pool put in about six months after Maggie was born and the kids were good swimmers because of it.

His face lit up. "Oh, definitely."

He stood up and yelled out to the kids, who were playing in the shade of the huge central tree. "Who wants to go swimming?"

"Me!" They both cried and ran for their father.

He leaned down and scooped them up into his arms, chatting animatedly as they told him about their morning.

Leo popped off my boob, his little milk drunk face absolutely perfect.

I put him over my shoulder and gently rubbed his back so he'd burp.

"Their swimmers are in the chest next to the door, hon," I said, knowing he was completely capable of looking after them.

He winked at me and set off to get them ready for a swim with him.

"How was the meeting this morning?" I asked, since he'd just arrived back from a quick trip to the office.

It was a Saturday and although Axel had slowed down so much in the past five years, he still did the occasional weekend or all-nighter. Not today, though.

"Fine," he said. "Pat had some strategies he wanted to go over, which were all good. He said they'll be over later for cake and maybe dinner. I was thinking of ordering in Chinese, if you want?"

I grinned at him. "I love that idea. Thank you."

It was Maggie's fifth birthday, but we'd gone low-key this year. With Leo just born, and Maggie due to start school next year, we'd decided to just have a cake and a chill night with our closest family.

"Great. I'll text him to confirm," Axel said and began getting the kids into their swimmers.

I lay back in the lounge with the baby over my shoulder and marveled at how amazing our life now was.

Axel had lessened his expectations of his duties and had gone into more of a co-executive role with my dad. They worked together on an equal standing, and Axel shared his old responsibilities.

He was happy, healthy, and slept eight hours most nights.

He was also the most incredible father. Attentive, patient, calm and present.

I watched in awe as he opened the gate to the pool and jumped in with the kids. Maggie was a proficient swimmer already and although Thomas was confident, he still swam with his floaties and vest on.

They splashed and played, and I leaned back in the lounge enjoying the warmth of the baby on my chest, moving his little sleeping form lower so I could cuddle him properly.

I'd never thought I could be this content and happy. It was an amazing feeling.

A few hours later, the kids had been bathed and were now dressed in their party clothes. For Maggie, that was a princess tutu dress with rainbow sparkles.

For Thomas, it was a spiderman costume, and I wasn't fighting either of them on their choices. They looked utterly adorable and it was, after all, their party.

The doorbell rang and Axel trotted off to open the door for my parents. I'd put out a few platters of food, and Maggie's cake was front and center. A princess castle cake, three tiers high, just like she wanted.

"Auntie C!" Grayson cried, running full tilt into the kitchen to greet me.

"Mr. Grayson!" I cried back, scooping up the gorgeous little brother that I adored with all my soul. "How are you doing today?"

"Great!" he said, looking pleased. "I made Maggie a card. Wanna see?" He held up the piece of paper with perfect little squiggly drawings all over it.

"That's perfect, buddy. How about you go show her?" I set Grayson down on the ground and he took off to find the other kids.

The three of them got along famously and it made our lives so much easier.

Mom walked into the room carrying two bottles of white wine, one in each hand. "I know you can't drink, but I need one," she announced, setting them both on the kitchen counter.

I laughed at her dramatic expression and pulled out a glass for her. "Why? What's wrong?"

She shook her head and slid onto the kitchen stool. "Oh, nothing. Grayson is the most healthy, energetic boy the pediatrician has ever seen. Perfect bill of health."

And yet my mother looked miserable.

"Then why do you look like you sucked on a lemon?" I opened the bottle of wine and poured her a glass.

She picked the glass up by the stem and took a sip. "Because I'm exhausted. He runs me off my feet every day."

I sighed. "He goes to school next year. Things will get easier."

"Yeah. Probably." She drank some more, and I sighed. Maggie was energetic but also liked to color and paint, be quiet and read. Boys weren't like that, and I could imagine that by the time Thomas was her age, I'd be praying for school to start too.

My father came into the kitchen and gave me a hug, a pink box tucked under his arm. "Where's my little princess?"

"Here I am, Papa!" Maggie cried, waving her arm madly.

Dad grinned at me and went off looking for her.

I stared after him, grinning at the picture they made together. Papa and his own little girl.

"She's surrounded by boys," I said, nodding at Maggie with her brother, her uncle and her grandfather.

Mom turned to look at the three kids playing on the mat. "They're perfect. And speaking of perfect, where's Leo?"

"In his bassinet," I said, nodding towards his room.

Mom hopped up and headed towards her newest grandchild, wine forgotten.

I shook my head and grabbed a bottle of water from the fridge. My mother may complain about how energetic the kids were, but she was great with them. She even had Maggie and Thomas over at her place once or twice a week, just so I could do my errands.

We'd fallen into a great pattern, my parents and I, especially with them living only about a ten-minute drive further out of the city. We caught up every week socially, shared childcare, and Dad and Axel worked together still.

Everything had turned out so much better than expected, even if Grayson was wearing my mom out.

"How about we do the cake?" I called out to the group, and everyone responded with cheering.

"Great." I grabbed the lighter and headed over to the table while Maggie jumped up on the chair so she could blow the candles out. "Remember, it's Maggie's birthday. You can have a turn at the candles later," I reminded her brother and uncle Grayson—who we referred to as her cousin most of the time.

The semantics were just too complicated for five-year-olds.

Mom walked out of the nursery holding baby Leo in her arms and Axel stood at the other end of the table holding up his phone to take photos and a video… I hoped.

"Ready? Happy birthday to you…." We sang while Maggie, my gorgeous little blonde cherub, grinned like she was the luckiest girl on the planet. And she was.

She had a family that loved her more than anything, and she had a smile that could melt your soul.

The song ended and I leaned in to whisper, "Blow out the candles, baby girl."

She blew hard and got them all out in one shot. We all cheered, my dad clapping loudly, and the boys fussing to have another go at the candles.

"Okay, okay. Grayson's turn, then Thomas' turn, all right? Then we can cut the cake."

We had to do two more lightings and blowing out of the candles, by this stage I wasn't sure anyone would want to eat the cake, but the kids had a fabulous time anyway.

But since they insisted, I cut the cake up and served it to the kids only. Once they were finished and wiped down, we all sat outside on the deck to watch the kids playing under the tree and on the swings.

"Happy?" Axel asked, rubbing my hand from his place to my right.

I nodded. "So very much. Everything is just perfect."

Then Thomas screamed and Maggie yelled, and my parents went running to break up the next fight.

Perfect chaos, that was my life now. With my handsome husband, and brand new baby, things couldn't get any sweeter.

THE END

Thank you so much for reading the last story in Axel and Chastity's trilogy!
If you would like to hear more about my new releases, you can join my mailing list here:

http://madmimi.com/signups/
bae7ba6c2d994340825b30fe1e205e5e/join

If you enjoy sweeter heroines, billionaires and babies, I think you'd really enjoy 'Accidentally Pregnant.'
Read on for a sneak peek into the story.

Accidentally Pregnant
Preview

Chapter 1

Accidentally Pregnant

The hot Hawaiian breeze ruffled Samara Jenkin's hair, providing a small amount of relief from the sticky humidity at her neck. She waved her hands ineffectually over her face, trying to cool her heated cheeks.

Against all the promises she'd made to herself about taking this year off work, she'd accepted this job and was now paying for it.

"Argh. Just think of the money."

She crossed her arms over her chest and tapped her foot on the sidewalk as she waited for some assistance. The hotel's owners wanted an honest appraisal of the state of their business and a strategy to improve sales.

She already had a list as long as her arm. Where was the concierge? Where was the bell boy? Where the hell was any staff member at this supposedly five-star resort?

Ridiculous! No wonder they called me.

She exhaled sharply, blowing the hair out of her eyes as she looked up at the thirty-story building. Aesthetically, it could use some work. Peeling paint littered the side of every surface, cracked windows made her grimace with the safety hazard they caused, and the eaves needed some attention, but the old girl displayed great architecture and presence. So much potential.

Obviously, she was going to wait all day in the sun unless she did something herself to change it, which disappointed her. The owner knew she planned to be here today. She arrived on time. There was no excuse for her not to be greeted at least by *someone*.

She took a measured breath, trying to push down the rising tide of frustration. When her parents called to say they were at risk of losing their house between health issues and pending foreclosure, she'd been happy to help. But that meant the money she'd saved for this year was half gone, and this one job would refill her coffers.

So, be grateful to this client, not pissy.

Her foot tapped harder and faster against the concrete, increasing the tempo as each notch of her temper stoked higher. Her pointed, strappy shoes made a slapping noise that started to irritate even her. Sweat trickled down between her shoulder blades and she shivered against the disgusting feeling.

"Yuck. Enough."

She threw up her hands and grabbed her luggage. Her eyes narrowed on the entrance and she stalked toward the double glass doors at a determined pace. She skidded to a halt a mere inch from breaking her nose, her ankle twisting as she threw on the anchors too late. Pain seared around her foot as the cold glass kissed the very tip of her nose and she glared through the door, waiting for it to respond.

Nothing.

She stepped backward and forward again, looking up at the sensor above the door and waited.

They didn't open.

You're kidding me? Should I wave my hands in the air like a crazy person now?

She peered through the glass and saw a young man in uniform hurrying toward her. He appeared to press a button beside the door and whoosh, the doors opened and cool air brushed past her heated face, bringing with it a huge sigh of relief from her body.

"I am so sorry, ma'am. Can I help you with your bags?"

The youth, who had pimply skin and bright, happy eyes, did not deserve the extended list of complaints bubbling up on her tongue.

She took a deep breath and focused on what he could do for her. "Yes, you can. Please take my suitcases and I'd like to check in."

The bell boy, or maitre'd—she wasn't quite sure which role he filled since he appeared to be the only person working at the hotel—took her suitcases off her hands with a grabbing, fast motion. He then turned on his black shoes that squeaked as he walked and dragged her matching bags half off their wheels as he hurried back to the main reception. She cringed as she watched them teeter and bang against the marble floor.

She looked away, anger rising inside her gut to see her luggage get abused like that. But the last thing she wanted to do was start grumbling at the only staff member she'd met. Instead, she glanced around the huge room.

Her shoulders dropped and her hands unclenched as she marveled at the room in which she stood. So grand, with a beautiful mystique that only period hotels and houses possessed. This hotel reminded her of an old lady—she had great bones, but they were tired. She would fix that.

"Please come over."

Samara tried not to notice that he'd dropped her custom, monogrammed luggage near the elevator, and then had rushed over to the desk where a computer stood waiting.

"Your name, ma'am?"

She bit her lip for a moment. *Seriously? You've actually got other people booked to check in today?* She couldn't say the thought aloud, so instead dragged her manners out of the over-cooked soup they were swimming in. "Samara Jenkins."

He tapped away on the computer until he finally held out a plastic card to her with the hotel's brown emblem on it.

"Room 2002, ma'am. Level twenty, room two. One of our best suites. May I accompany you up?"

She waved her hands at him. If he left the foyer, who was going to let any other possible customers into the hotel? That broken glass door certainly wasn't going to just start working on its own. "No thanks, but can you bring up the larger suitcase in an hour or so?"

The stink of crowded planes and cars, and hours of waiting in the heat and humidity had all left a stain that needed to be washed away. Preferably somewhere quiet, where she could be alone and think for a minute.

Samara picked up her smaller suitcase, which contained a change of clothes and toiletries. A shower was definitely first priority on her list. With a determined clench of her jaw, she turned around and strode over to the lift, releasing a sigh when the doors dinged and opened. She wasn't walking up twenty flights of stairs.

She'd go home and damn the massive commission before that ever happened.

You need it, don't kid yourself.

A frown pulled down her lips. She'd had enough money for her plans, until her parents called with their life altering news. But not even a week after she'd handed over half her saving to her parents had fate delivered a favor in the form of a phone call from the matriarch of this hotel empire. Samara had been offered this job and it would replace all the money she'd lost with only a few weeks of work. As long as she delivered the results they wanted.

She could have tried to accomplish everything she wanted to do this year without the money, but their offer was far too good to turn down.

Stepping inside the elevator, she pressed the tip of her forefinger to the dusty button for the twentieth floor, gripping the rail. The moving box's cables screeched and moaned as it hauled her up the shaft. This elevator didn't look like it had been updated since the inception of the hotel. If the cables failed, or the electricity went out, she'd be stuck in the elevator without water for hours. Not a pleasant prospect in this heat. She grabbed for her bag to check if she had anything with her to survive such an event. The elevator ground to a clunking halt.

A squeak popped out of her throat, grabbing for the gold railing as the doors dinged open.

Oh, thank goodness for that. Something else to put on the list. Can't have the guests fearing for their lives every time they go back to their rooms.

Large blue eyes, set in a very handsome face, stared at her from the center of the hallway. "Miss Jenkins, I presume?" His cool, familiar New York tones straightened her spine.

"Hold the door for me would you, please?" She looked away from his intense gaze, arousal curling in her belly like an old, absent friend. She locked her hand into the handle on her small suitcase and took a shallow breath as he stepped close and did as she'd asked. Twisting his huge body to the side, he placed his arm out to stop the elevator door from closing on her.

His eyes followed her with an intensity that had her belly tightening and blood rushing through her nether regions. His face was cut like the smoothest stone, his strong and angular cheek bones reminding her of old roman warriors she'd once seen paintings of. Real men. Men that forced their enemies to their knees, and often, all the women around them too.

Her breath locked in her throat as she moved past him, the presence of his huge body in the door making heat warm her cheeks that had nothing to do with the summer air. She wasn't short by anyone's standard, but at five foot seven she was at least six inches shorter than he was. She felt like a dwarf facing a giant. Who was this? He knew her name, but how? It couldn't be the owner who had hired her, although he had the air of someone with money. A lot of money.

"Excuse me."

She stepped onto the landing and moved toward the door that had *2002* on the panel, trying very hard not to turn around and stare at the man behind her. Every cell in her body grew far too aware of him. The hairs stood up on her neck.

Professional, stay professional. Why did he have to be so gorgeous?

The man behind her had to be a manager of some sort. He was the only one she'd met so far who knew who she was, and he obviously had anticipated her arrival and had been waiting for her.

She placed her small suitcase and handbag against her room door, her skin tingling with the awareness of being watched. Then, when she was sure she had schooled her features into something resembling calm, she turned around, her heart leaping at the sight of the man behind her. He was so gorgeous. Tall, broad and with full lips that would curve beautifully when he eventually smiled. Her skin tingled from just looking at him.

She focused for a moment and dismissed the idea he was a manager. His suit was worth more than her wardrobe put together. And if that wasn't enough, the man in front of her had an arrogance in his posture that she'd come to see only from people born into wealth.

"Yes, I'm Samara Jenkins, and you are?" She squared her shoulder and stood facing the large man on the landing. His eyes were a startling blue, like a bright summer sky. With his dark-brown hair and fair skin, the combination was rare and beautiful. The saliva gathered in her mouth, making her swallow awkwardly.

"Julian King. My mother was the one that hired you."

Her eyes slid down his body, the breadth of his shoulders as impressive as any footballer's. His black suit appeared tailor made, beautiful in design, and comprised of strong lines that made him look like a panther about to pounce. She shivered at the thought.

"I'm sorry I didn't greet you downstairs, but I wanted you to experience the hotel as it currently is."

That explained a lot, although a touch of forewarning may not have gone astray. "We have a lot to discuss. I have a list a mile long already of things that need to be altered and implemented, and I haven't even stepped inside my room yet."

He chuckled, a soft earthy sound that surprised her. "I assure you that I have everything under control. You are here as an advisor, nothing more."

Ice slid on to her shoulders and she straightened her spine. That wasn't what she'd been told, but she'd gotten around difficult men before. Minding their fragile egos while doing her job was a specialty of hers. "I didn't realize that was what I had agreed to, Mr. King."

His lips tilted up into a soft smile as though he agreed with her. "I was told you were the best, although I didn't expect you to be quite so young."

There was a tone of admiration and reluctant respect in his voice that pleased her. It tickled right along her spine. She'd heard that a lot over the past ten years, and she always enjoyed her clients surprise when she exceeded their expectations. She was good at her job, and her age had nothing to do with it. The original trouble she'd had starting her business only meant she'd increased her commission to prove she was worth it.

"I didn't expect you at all, Mr. King." When she'd pictured who she was going to meet on arriving, she'd envisioned either the elderly woman who'd hired her over the phone, or perhaps the manager.

He inclined his head with a more natural smile flirting on his lips. "Touché. Let's meet downstairs in fifteen minutes."

Samara checked her watch. It may be dinner time here but in New York it was going on 2 am. No wonder her eyes were tired and her neck ached. She'd barely slept on the plane.

"Make it an hour, if possible. Where shall I meet you?"

His flaring nostrils was the only give away that she had displeased him, but she stood her ground, calmly waiting for his response while fanning her face with her hand. It was way too hot in this hotel for comfort.

"The hotel's restaurant for dinner. It's on the ground floor."

Perfect place to start.

She could definitely eat something, although she didn't have much of an appetite after traveling all day. She nodded at him to agree, although her head swam from fatigue and something else she couldn't quite put her finger on.

"See you in one hour, Miss Jenkins."

He turned and strode toward the lift. Samara couldn't stop her eyes from dropping down to drift over his body as he moved away. Her hungry gaze devoured his angles as he put both hands in his pants pockets, pulling the jacket up and stretching it tight across his rounded butt.

She bit her lip as she looked her fill, desire fluttering low in her belly. He had the perfect arse, long legs, a tapered waist and huge, broad shoulders. The combination was heady indeed. He was definitely one of the most imposing men she'd ever seen in real life.

A tailored suit made most men look good, but this one actually seemed to hamper his beauty. She could sense the power leashed beneath that black cloth, and she could only imagine how amazing he'd look without the modern armor.

The old elevator dinged and groaned as it opened and Samara sighed as she pushed her way into her room, letting perhaps the most breath-taking man she'd ever seen slip from her mind. His hotel rooms needed to be at the forefront of her racing brain and that was how it would stay.

Unlike everything else she'd seen so far in the hotel, the card the clerk had given her was at least new. She had to concentrate with the man behind her causing an unusual breathlessness in her chest, but she managed to slide the plastic into the lock shaft.

She waited. She glanced up at the door. Nothing. Her eyes flicked up to the number on the door. Yes, it was the right room. So she jiggled it until the red light eventually turned green.

How can they charge people three hundred dollars a night if the keys don't even work?

She pushed open the door with one hand and dragged her suitcase in with the other.

The bell boy had been right. Her suite was massive and would have been very grand once upon a time, but the room hadn't been aired out in weeks. A musky, damp smell curled up her nostrils that would put off anyone who liked clean air.

Gross.

She placed her small luggage by the wardrobe and raced over to the window, pushing open the sliding glass and allowing some of the humid, but fresh air into the room. Inhaling a few good lungful's, she grabbed the courage to turn back around and inspect the rest of the room.

The king-sized bed was in the right place. Small, cheap looking nightstands framed the bed, disappointing her. The bed covers didn't suit the color of the walls, but overall, it wasn't too bad decor. For a three-star hotel.

She snorted and marched over to the bathroom. This would be the test. Pulling open the door, she gagged for breath as the stale smell of urine, bleach, and hot, pungent air took flight inside her throat.

"Holy mother of...." She rushed back to the window, opening every glass pane that would open. She took several slow breaths, her mind whirling with the work before her. Grass roots job this was. Cleaning staff, decoration, the whole lot, and *then* she'd see if the gorgeous Mr. King had what it took to get his hotel back up to the standard that it deserved.

SHE WAS SO MUCH MORE BEAUTIFUL THAN HE'D EXPECTED. IT WAS TRUE, those that had raved of her characteristics often threw words around like gorgeous, stunning and lovely into their appraisals, but he'd taken it with the mountain of salt he'd thought it deserved.

He'd been wrong. And he wasn't often wrong.

Surprising, for sure, that the woman his parents had lumbered him with for a fortnight, was so lovely to look at. He didn't want help, hadn't asked for it, nor did he think he needed it. He took full responsibility for the state the hotel presented currently. He'd hired an executive manager two years ago to oversee the hotels every day running, and he'd been very, very wrong in his estimation of Kostas Dean. A villain, pure and simple.

When Julian's marriage ended and he'd needed time away from business, Kostas stepped up. But instead of looking after his company the way Julian expected, Kostas had siphoned money, hidden the complaints, and threatened senior management with job loss if they dared step out of line.

They were in a lot of trouble by the time Julian came back to his senses and picked up his role again.

Kostas was missing, with several million dollars of their money.

But he'd be found. Eventually.

Julian glanced down at his watch just as the second hand ticked toward the number twelve. An hour had passed since he'd seen Miss Samara Jenkins. The door to the restaurant opened and then clicked shut again. A smile tugged at Julian's lips. *On time to the second.*

She walked toward him, her thin, plain blue cotton dress clinging to her lush curves. Where was the battle armor that he'd come to expect with business women? She wore natural makeup that accentuated her pretty face, and her entire ensemble had a relaxed holiday feel about it that he hadn't expected. She wore flat shoes, her hair down, and no jewelry.

Samara Jenkins had a body that would look spectacular naked and stretched across his bed. Long hair that would cover her full breasts like a silky curtain, and lips that would be perfect to kiss. He raised his eyes from the full curve of her mouth to make eye-contact and her fresh face hit him right in the gut.

They'd lied about her being beautiful.

Breath taking seemed far more apt.

Samara pulled out the chair and took the seat opposite him. "This hotel is in dire straits. I don't think I've ever seen anything so bad before."

The smile that had been playing at his lips as he'd imagined her naked converted into a tight frown. He cleared his throat and shifted in his chair, unable to simply just take her criticism. He opened his mouth to defend his hotel, then snapped it shut again.

She has a point.

Three months more of the current climate and he'd have to shut the hotel down to sit here and rot. He would never allow that to happen on his watch, and although he didn't require her help, she was here. He would be stupid indeed not to take advantage of it. "What do you suggest, Miss Jenkins?"

She grinned at him with sunny warmth and picked up the menu. "That's the spirit. I like it. Can we order first?" She glanced down into her menu. Her mouth tweaked up at the corners as she read, her happy face at odds with the churning in Julian's guts. What was wrong with him?

Samara lifted her head and swiveled like a bird, eyes alert and neck straight. "Where are the staff? This is the hotel's five-star restaurant, is it not?"

That twist in his belly rolled some more as his cheeks flared with heat. Each sentence she uttered reminded him of how badly he'd failed in his job of maintaining his family's holdings. How much work this hotel actually needed to get it back to the standard it had once boasted. She was the salt in a very large wound, and to make matters worse, his own mother had been the one throwing the salt.

He lifted his hand and indicated to the man lolling around in the corner of the room. The youth sashayed over, his hips taking on a music of their own.

"Yeah?" the waiter asked him.

A little giggle burst from Samara's mouth. "Ooh, we are in some serious trouble."

"I'll have the steak," Julian ground out, glaring at the youth until he looked at the carpet. Samara's relaxed attitude grated on his nerves. This was serious. They were losing tens of thousands by the day and she was giggling her way through dinner. Why the hell had his mother hired this woman?

Because she's the best, they all said it. Just wait! You can't afford for any of this to go wrong.

"And you, ma'am?" the waiter asked, inclining his head towards Samara.

Finally, some manners.

"I'll have the garlic shrimps for entree, the fillet steak for main and the chocolate soufflé for dessert."

The waiter's eyes bulged a little at her order, but he pulled out his pen and pad from his pocket and wrote it all down, Julian hoped, correctly.

Samara's keen eyes watched the waiter as he walked away and then gave Julian a pointed stare as though trying to communicate without words just how bad the service was. Anger rolled in his belly like a storm cloud, his hands fisting on the white tablecloth as he maintained eye contact with her green gaze. He'd thought he'd be prepared for how badly the hotel would fare under the stare of a professional, but he had been grossly mistaken.

Pride warred with stubborn arrogance. Maybe, just maybe, he could use her to help. He was surprised by her order but didn't say anything. Either she was hungry after her journey, or she was testing out the skills of his cook. He was impressed either way. Bird-like salads were no way to eat, for anyone.

Her lips twisted up into a grimace. "No drinks order and he didn't ask how I wanted my steak cooked… Interesting."

Julian nodded once in acceptance of her complaint. Too true.

When the incompetent waiter finally left, Julian grabbed for his water, gulping down some of the cold liquid as his aching throat cried out for it. When he placed it down, some of his thirst quenched, Samara's cool green eyes continued to stare at him.

"Start from the beginning, Mr. King, and tell me how this happened."

Julian took a moment, and a long breath, to consider how much he should tell her. He didn't want her help. But she was here and he would consider what she had to say. His mother was paying her to consult for them, and before all of this, that would have been enough.

However, she didn't need to know *everything*. "All right, Miss Jenkins. As my mother would have told you over the phone, my family owns a chain of hotels all over the world. Over the past year, their management had become increasingly questionable." And his parents would never forgive him for screwing his way through Europe instead of being at home, running the company, while his legacy fell apart. The worst part was, that he'd bribed most of the executive managers to hide what he was doing. His treachery had reached far and wide. "All the other hotels had good enough staff to survive the storm and since we found who'd been syphoning money, the bleeding has stopped. We are re-building. New managers have been hired and the other hotels are thriving. This one however, is not. Despite us hiring the best local manager we could find. That is why I am here…." He chewed on the inside of his cheek. "And the reason I believe my mother hired you. She was told that you have an exceptional brain for analyzing what any business needs, if you indeed have it."

She didn't respond to his back handed compliment except to bite on her lip in the most adorable way that made him want to lean in and take over with his own mouth.

"Is there any particular reason why the management of your hotel became questionable?"

He clenched his teeth together and inhaled through his nose. It hurt, like picking at a sore to be admitting this to her, but he was an adult, and responsible for his own actions. "I wasn't paying attention as I should have been. Personal reasons."

She gave him a soft smile that did nothing to maintain the ice around his heart.

"I won't ask you what sort of personal reasons, Mr. King, it is none of my business, but I am going to assume such problems are behind you?"

Bloody hell, yes.

He nodded once and she continued. "From what I've seen, we'll need months to get this hotel back to a standard that can be classed as five star, but I don't have that much time."

"Yes, *your* personal reasons."

"Just so." She inclined her head again, a mutual respect for their private lives firmly in place. His mother had made it clear that she was only available for two weeks. It had been one of the only reasons he had allowed his parent going over his head and hiring a consultant to help him. He wouldn't have to deal with her interference for very long.

Just think of her as an overqualified assistant, and fix up this mess, Julian. The last words his mother had said to him, over a week ago.

"However, I will give you these two weeks, Mr. King, and I promise to work my absolute hardest to put into place everything you will need. Once I am done, do you have strategies in place to get people back to the hotel?"

He nodded firmly, reluctantly impressed with her. She was right, two weeks was not long enough to get everything done that needed to be done, but if he decided that she'd be of use to him, he would change her mind. She'd stay. He'd make sure of it.

However, she'd made a valid point. Many people had been driven away by the declining standards of the hotel, and it was his main job to do everything in his power to get people back onto the grounds. But that meant he needed someone else manning the changes to the actual hotel.

Damn. Mom might actually be right about this one.

"Yes, Ms. Jenkins. I have a marketing expert on standby and several conferences already booked for next month. The one advantage we have is that we are one of the few hotels on the island with large facilities and the rooms to house several hundred people."

"Fantastic."

Her shrimp arrived and they looked and smelled great. His stomach grumbled in preparation for his own meal.

"Presentation is respectable, but I would expect less shrimp on the plate, and more color in an entree." She took a forkful of rice and ate a single shrimp. *Just one?* "They are cooked… all right, although I believe you will need to hire a head chef to take over from the current one."

"You can tell that already?"

She blinked once, her eyes wide as they stared at him. "Of course. I spent several years training with five-star restaurants and all of their staff. Chefs in particular. This is not up to the standard in taste, texture, or design. If you want people to pay twenty odd dollars for an entree, you better make sure it's up to par."

She had his curiosity well and sincerely hooked. "Why a head chef specifically?"

"Because it's obvious that you have a cook posing as the head chef in your kitchen that is probably trying their best, but they don't have the training, nor the skills. A proper head chef will organize the staff, train them, and add the correct flair to each dish. You won't need much more staff in the kitchen I don't believe, although of course I will assess that when I go in."

She called the waiter over. "Thank you. May I have the main meal now please?"

Julian sat in awe watching her, the cool confidence, the girl next door beauty. Her brain appeared to work faster than anyone he'd ever met, and her earthiness was as refreshing as her simple clothes. "What else do you suggest?"

She sat up straighter, a grin stretching across her pink glossed lips. "Firstly, we need to get in a decorator. Tomorrow preferably. The rooms aren't terrible, but they all need better linens, painting, and a very thorough cleaning at the very least."

He kept his tone calm and raised one eyebrow. Did she want him to pick the hotel up and move it closer to the beach too? "That's all?"

She laughed. "You joke, but the list I have is huge. I need to interview every staff member and probably double the cleaning crew. This whole hotel needs maintenance. We need to hire a concierge and a proper manager. I assume there is one at the moment, although I have yet to meet them, but if they are in the same boat as the rest of the staff, then they need some serious re-training too."

He cleared his throat. "I found the executive manager siphoning money from the hotel like many of the others. I fired him a few weeks ago. The local manager is not up to speed, you are quite right about that, so I will be hiring a new one."

Their main meals arrived and Samara did a similar analysis, sampling everything on her plate, making similar comments, and then asking for the meal to be taken away.

Julian ate his steak while she talked about the amenities, the website, everything. He rarely felt out of depth with a person, in fact, from all his years in private school, college, university and then the corporate world, he'd never had an experience like this one. A literal whirl wind of information, design and strategy. If she was half as efficient and effective as she seemed to be, he'd have his family's hotel back on track in no time.

When dessert arrived, she sighed dramatically. "Now this is what I'm talking about."

"Why? Because it has cream and a mint leaf?"

The meal appeared dressed better than all the other meals, but he was by no means a food critic.

"That is an answer that is hard to explain to anyone who doesn't love chocolate as much as I do."

She took a bite and moaned, her eyes sliding closed in bliss. That primitive sound shot straight to his groin, hot blood throbbing along his cock as he imagined Samara beneath him making those same sounds. He bit back his own groan and looked away, unable to hide the effect she was having on him.

He needed a woman, and fast. It had been too long for him, obviously. Embarrassment bloomed into anger in his gut. Time to cut this meeting short and go back to his own room for a long, hot shower.

"I want a report on my desk by tomorrow morning. Good night Miss Jenkins." He stood up and Samara gaped up at him. A twang of guilt hit him in the chest, but he pushed it away just as fast.

"Did I say something wrong?"

He tugged at his cufflinks and straightened his jacket, a cool breeze filling his throat and not allowing any warmth into his tone. "No, of course not. But there's lots to do and not much time to do it in."

She put her spoon down, her eyes showing confusion in their green depths. "All right. I'll put everything down for you."

His shoulders tightened with unease as he fought the need to apologize, sit down, and drown in her eyes once again. But that's not what he was here to do.

"Sleep well, Ms. Jenkins."

"Good night, Mr. King."

My newsletter is : HERE